TOO LATE

Jessica felt instant panic. What if Mr. Hopper had already left? She'd never be able to give him the money! She ran full speed to the front porch and rang the doorbell anxiously. No one answered.

"Now what?" Jessica muttered under her breath. She plopped down onto the step dejectedly.

"Might you be Miss Wakefield?"

Jessica glanced up to see an older gray-haired man with a cane, approaching her slowly. "Yes," she answered with a spark of hope. "My father sent me over to deliver something to Mr. Hopper." She stood up, still holding the envelope full of money for the charitable fund.

"I'm Mr. Roberts," the man said. "Jim Hopper's next-door neighbor. He asked me to keep an eye out for you. Jim waited for you as long as he could, but then he had to leave for a dinner appointment."

Jessica's heart sank. She was too late. As soon as her father found out about this, she would definitely be in trouble. Big trouble. . . .

Bantam Books in the SWEET VALLEY TWINS series
Ask your bookseller for the books you have missed

Sweet Valley Twins Super Editions

Sweet Valley Twins Super Chiller

SWEET VALLEY TWINS

Jessica and the Money Mix-Up

◇

Written by
Jamie Suzanne

Created by
FRANCINE PASCAL

BANTAM BOOKS
NEW YORK · TORONTO · LONDON · SYDNEY · AUCKLAND

RL 4, 008–012

JESSICA AND THE MONEY MIX-UP
A Bantam Skylark Book / May 1990

Sweet Valley High® and Sweet Valley Twins are trademarks of
Francine Pascal

Conceived by Francine Pascal

Produced by Daniel Weiss Associates, Inc.
33 West 17th Street
New York, NY 10011

Cover art by James Mathewuse

ISBN 0-553-15798-1

Published simultaneously in the United States and Canada

Bantam Books are published by Bantam Books, a division of Bantam
Doubleday Dell Publishing Group, Inc. Its trademark, consisting of the
words "Bantam Books" and the portrayal of a rooster, is Registered in
U.S. Patent and Trademark Office and in other countries. Marca
Registrada. Bantam Books, 666 Fifth Avenue, New York, New York
10103.

PRINTED IN THE UNITED STATES OF AMERICA

O   0 9 8 7 6 5 4

One

◇

"I don't have anything to wear roller-skating!" Jessica Wakefield moaned. She stared forlornly at the clothes hanging in her bedroom closet.

Her twin sister, Elizabeth, couldn't help but giggle. "Somehow I find that hard to believe." She shoved aside the pile of clothing on Jessica's bed and sat down. "What happened to my pink blouse?"

"Pink blouse?" Jessica echoed.

"The one you borrowed the day before yesterday," Elizabeth reminded her.

"Oh. *That* pink blouse," Jessica said lightly.

"I was going to wear it to school Monday with my new jean skirt," Elizabeth added, studying her sister suspiciously.

"You know what would look even better?" Jessica's blue-green eyes lit up with sudden inspiration. "My new red T-shirt. The one I just bought at Kendell's. You can borrow it if you want."

Elizabeth crossed her arms over her chest and looked at her twin. "Jess, is there something you're not telling me about my blouse?"

Jessica flipped her long blond hair back over one shoulder. "I was just trying to be helpful," she said innocently.

"If you want to be helpful, you might start by cleaning up the bathroom," Elizabeth suggested. "It looks like it was hit by a tornado."

"Don't worry about the bathroom, Liz," Jessica said. "I'll have it cleaned up before Mom gets back from her trip."

"You think a week will give you enough time?" Elizabeth teased.

Mrs. Wakefield worked as a part-time interior designer. She was away on business in San Francisco for the week. While she was gone, the twins and their fourteen-year-old brother, Steven, were supposed to help Mr. Wakefield keep the house running smoothly.

Jessica hadn't been much help with the housework, but then, that was hardly surprising. Even though Jessica was only four minutes younger than her sister, sometimes it seemed more like four years. It was often hard to believe they were identical twins.

On the outside, Elizabeth and Jessica were mirror images. Both twins had long, sun-streaked blond hair, blue-green eyes, and wore the same size clothing. They even had the same dimple that showed in their left cheeks whenever they smiled.

But when it came to their personalities, the twins were very different. Elizabeth liked to read, and her dream was to become a professional journalist someday. She devoted a lot of time to working on *The Sweet Valley Sixers*, the sixth-grade newspaper. Her best friends, Amy Sutton and Julie Porter, also worked on the paper. Occasionally Elizabeth liked to spend time alone, reading a book or just thinking. And Elizabeth loved school— even the difficult subjects like math.

Jessica liked school, too, but her favorite part of the day was lunchtime. That's when she sat with all her friends and gossiped about clothes and boys, two of her favorite topics. She was a member of the Unicorns, a group of the most popular girls at Sweet Valley Middle School. Elizabeth thought the "Snob Squad," her nickname for the Unicorn Club, was silly and that the things they liked to do were boring. But Jessica always had fun when she was with them, and to Jessica, having fun was the most important thing in the world. Frequently, the fun-loving schemes she cooked up got her into trouble, but she knew she could always count on Elizabeth to help bail her out.

She hoped Elizabeth was in an especially understanding mood right now.

Elizabeth was still watching Jessica suspiciously. "Jessica," she said, "did something happen to my blouse? You may as well just tell me."

Reluctantly, Jessica went into the bathroom and retrieved Elizabeth's crumpled pink blouse from the clothes hamper. There, on the front of the blouse, was a large brown splotch.

"Jessica!" Elizabeth cried. "What *happened*?"

"Really, it wasn't my fault, Lizzie," Jessica blurted out. "I was making a chocolate sundae after school and the phone rang and when I went to grab it, the chocolate sauce sort of . . . well—"

"—spilled." Elizabeth finished her sister's sentence. "Oh, Jess, why didn't you at least wipe it off? Now it might never come clean."

"I was hoping Mom would take care of it when she got back," Jessica said lamely. "Suppose I set the table *and* clear the dishes tonight to make it up to you?"

Elizabeth still looked unhappy.

"OK," Jessica said with a shrug. "Tonight and tomorrow night."

Elizabeth slowly broke into a smile. It was awfully hard to stay mad at Jessica. "Three nights," she bargained. "Plus the bathroom, before Mom gets home."

Jessica wrinkled her nose. "All right, big sister. It's a deal." She turned her attention back to her closet. "Now, have you got any suggestions on what I can wear roller-skating tonight?"

"Wear anything," Elizabeth said with a sly grin. "As long as it isn't mine!" She hopped off the bed and headed toward the door. "I'm on my way over to Amy's now, but I'll be back before dinner. Don't forget, Dad is working in his study."

Mr. Wakefield, who was a lawyer, had been working very hard on a big project. With Mrs. Wakefield out of town and the extra pressures of his job, he grew grumpier by the minute. Everybody had been walking on tiptoes, trying not to bother him.

"Steven's outside playing basketball. I think he's trying to stay out of Dad's way," Elizabeth continued.

"OK," Jessica said absently. She was still concentrating on her closet. "Have fun at Amy's."

After Elizabeth left, Jessica spent a few more minutes trying on outfits. Nothing seemed quite right, so she decided to check the laundry room. Maybe she had forgotten all about some terrific outfit hiding in the dryer.

Jessica rushed all the way down to the basement only to be disappointed. Nothing but towels were in the dryer. Glumly, she trudged back up the stairs to the kitchen. Suddenly it hit her. She knew just whom to call to help her with her wardrobe problem. When it came to clothes, Jessica's friend Lila Fowler was definitely an expert. She would know exactly how to handle Jessica's dilemma. Lila's father was one of the wealthiest men in Sweet Valley, and he spoiled his daughter to make up for all the time he spent away on business trips. There was no one in Sweet Valley who had a bigger or more current wardrobe than Lila.

Jessica tiptoed over to her father's study and peeked in the half-open door. Mr. Wakefield was flipping through a thick law book while he spoke to someone on the phone.

She waited outside the door until she heard him hang up. Then she rushed upstairs to the phone in the hallway and dialed Lila's number.

"Help!" Jessica cried as soon as Lila answered the phone. "What should I wear tonight?"

"How about something padded?" Lila suggested with a giggle. "Just in case you fall down."

"Very funny, Lila," Jessica. "This is serious!"

An hour later, Jessica finally hung up the phone. She had decided to wear her stone-washed jeans and a yellow T-shirt. She was in the midst of putting on her jeans when the phone rang again. *That's probably Lila again*, she thought to herself.

She ran out into the hall and picked up the phone. Usually Jessica answered the phone by saying "Wakefield residence," but she was so sure that it was Lila on the other end, she decided to surprise her.

"Hi, Lila," she said into the receiver.

There was a brief silence on the other end. Then she heard a man's startled deep voice. "Oh, I'm sorry," he said. "I was trying to reach Ned Wakefield."

"This is his house," Jessica said, feeling a bit embarrassed. "Just a second, please. I'll go get him."

She rushed downstairs to his study. "Dad?" she called through the half-open door. "Telephone."

"Thanks, Jess," he responded.

Jessica went up to her room. She was searching through the mountain of clothes on her bed for a pair of socks when she heard her father's voice.

"Jessica, I'd like to speak to you," he called sternly. "Right away."

Jessica froze. Her father sounded angry. "Coming, Dad," she answered, flying back down the stairs.

The door to Mr. Wakefield's study was all the way open now. He sat in his big leather chair, tapping his pencil. There were papers and manila folders spread all over his desk. One look at his face told Jessica all she needed to know.

"That was Mr. Leeds on the phone," he said slowly. "He's been trying to reach me for forty-five minutes with some very important information."

Jessica had a feeling she knew what was coming next.

"But every time he tried our number, the line was busy." Mr. Wakefield folded his hands on top of his desk. "I don't suppose you have any idea why he couldn't get through?"

"Well . . ." Jessica hesitated. "I was talking to Lila for a little while."

"A *little* while?" Mr. Wakefield repeated skeptically, raising an eyebrow.

"We were talking about going roller-skating tonight, and I guess I forgot that you might need to use the phone," Jessica went on.

As soon as the words *roller-skating* were out of her mouth, Jessica regretted it. This probably wasn't a very good time to bring up skating. Especially since she was in very real danger of being grounded for a very long time.

But Mr. Wakefield smiled. "I understand that it can be hard on you and your sister when your mother's away and I'm working overtime. But I need to know I can count on you to behave responsibly, Jess."

"I know, Daddy." Jessica stared at the floor. "I'm really sorry."

"The past couple of weeks haven't exactly been your finest," her father continued. "I'm sure I don't have to remind you about that D you got on your history test last week."

Jessica felt her face flush. Technically, it was not her fault that she had done so poorly. The day before that test, she had bought the brand-new Johnny Buck album, *Pass the Buck*. It was only natural that she had spent the whole evening listening to it instead of studying. By the next morning she had memorized all the words to Johnny's newest hit song, "Rockin' Steady." Unfortunately, there hadn't been even one question about Johnny Buck on her history exam, and there had only been two questions she knew the answer to.

"I promise I'll do better, Dad," she pleaded in her best you-can-trust-me voice. "I'm going to get an A in history next time, and I'll be sure all my phone calls last less than a minute."

For a brief moment, Mr. Wakefield smiled. "That'll be the day," he murmured. He rubbed his eyes and his grin disappeared.

Jessica felt terrible. This certainly was not the first time she had gotten into trouble, but her father had never lost faith in her before.

"Please give me a chance to prove myself, Dad," she said earnestly. "I promise, you won't be disappointed." She pointed to the stack of papers on his desk. "I could help you with your work, if you like."

Mr. Wakefield shook his head. "I don't think so, Jess." He reached for the phone. "I've got to get back to work. We can talk more about this at dinner."

"Sure, Dad," Jessica whispered, leaving his office quietly. *Maybe if I go straight to the kitchen and set the table, it will help*, she thought hopefully.

Jessica had just set down the last plate when she looked up to see her father entering the kitchen. He was carrying a small brown envelope.

"Jessica, I have a favor to ask of you," he announced. "Perhaps this will give you a chance to prove you can act responsibly. This envelope has five hundred dollars in it," Mr. Wakefield explained. "It's money I've been collecting at work for a local charity fund. I have to deliver it to Mr. Hopper, the group's treasurer, before he goes on vacation. He's leaving tomorrow morning and he'll be gone for a week. I'd like to get this to him today. He lives three blocks down, over on Walnut Street."

"I'll take it over, Dad," Jessica volunteered eagerly.

"I just spoke with Mr. Hopper on the telephone. He's home now, packing for his trip," her father said. "I'd like you to take it over to him right away. His address is on the envelope." Mr. Wakefield gave her a serious look. "It's a lot of money, but I know I can trust you."

"No problem," Jessica told him with complete confidence. She took the envelope from her father's hand. "I'll be back before you know it."

"Thanks, Jess. I really appreciate it," Mr. Wakefield said.

A few minutes later Jessica was walking briskly toward Walnut Street. *I sure got off easily this time*, she thought with a sense of accomplishment. *What could possibly go wrong in three blocks?*

Two

◇

The late afternoon sun was still warm as Jessica walked toward Mr. Hopper's house. She had just turned onto Walnut Street when she saw Caroline Pearce riding by on her bike.

"Hello, Jessica!" Caroline yelled.

Jessica kept walking. She wanted to finish her errand as quickly as possible.

"Hey, Jessica!" Caroline called. She stopped her bike near the curb where Jessica was walking. "Slow down a minute, I want to tell you something."

"I can't," Jessica told her. "I'm running an urgent errand for my father," she added importantly.

"Really?" Caroline asked, her green eyes widening. "Sounds very interesting." Caroline was the gossip columnist for *The Sweet Valley Sixers*. It was the perfect job for her, since she was the nosiest person in Sweet Valley. "What's in the envelope?" she asked.

"Can't tell you," Jessica replied mysteriously.

Caroline looked a little disappointed. "Well, even if you *won't* tell me anything," she whispered, "I've got something to tell you." She leaned closer. "It concerns a certain seventh-grader whose initials just happen to be B.P."

Jessica's mouth dropped open. "Bruce Patman?" she asked. "What about him?"

"I have very reliable sources," Caroline told her. "And they say Bruce is actually taking a date skating tonight!"

"A date?" Jessica echoed in amazement. "You mean he's taking a *girl*?"

"No, Jessica, I mean a guy," Caroline answered sarcastically. "Of *course* I mean a girl!"

"But who?" Jessica demanded. She couldn't wait to tell Lila about it. Bruce Patman was the cutest and most popular boy in the seventh grade.

Caroline tucked a strand of long red hair behind her ear. "Actually, it's a long story," she began to explain.

Jessica sighed. With Caroline *everything* was a long story. And it was always hard to know how much of it to believe.

For a moment, Jessica hesitated. After all, she *was* in a bit of a hurry. But she was certain a few minutes wouldn't hurt. She would just get the scoop on Bruce, and then be on her way. It was only a half block more to Mr. Hopper's house.

"OK," Jessica said. "Tell me all the details."

Caroline climbed off her bike and sat on the curb. Jessica sat down, too. For the next half hour they discussed who Bruce might bring skating. Unfortunately, Caroline seemed to have no idea who the lucky girl would be.

Suddenly Jessica glanced down at the envelope in her hands. She had completely forgotten about Mr. Hopper!

"Oh, no!" she exclaimed. She jumped to her feet.

"What's the matter?" Caroline asked curiously.

"I forgot all about my errand," Jessica cried. She checked the address on the envelope. "J. Hopper," it read. "Thirty-seven Walnut Street."

Jessica began racing down the street. "Gotta go," she called over her shoulder.

Caroline shrugged and waved. "Have fun tonight," she called back.

At last Jessica arrived at Thirty-seven Walnut Street. But there were no lights on inside. Worse yet, the driveway was empty.

Jessica panicked. What if Mr. Hopper had already left?

She ran full speed to the front porch and rang the doorbell anxiously. No one answered. She rang again. Still no answer.

"Now what?" Jessica muttered under her breath. She plopped down onto the step dejectedly. What would she tell her father?

"Might you be Miss Wakefield?"

Jessica glanced up to see a gray-haired man with a cane approaching her.

"Yes," she answered with a spark of hope. She stood up, still holding the envelope full of money.

"I'm Mr. Roberts," the man said. "Jim Hopper's next-door neighbor. He asked me to keep an eye out for you."

Jessica smiled with relief. Maybe she hadn't messed things up, after all.

"Jim waited for you as long as he could," Mr. Roberts continued. "But then he had to leave for a dinner appointment."

Jessica's heart sank. She was too late.

"He tried to call your house to tell your father, but the phone was busy."

Thank heavens for that! Jessica thought to herself. At least her father didn't know what had happened yet.

"Thank you, sir," she murmured under her breath.

"My pleasure." The old man gave a little bow and headed down the driveway.

Jessica followed behind him defeatedly. There was no doubt in her mind. As soon as her father found out about this, she would definitely be in trouble. Big trouble.

But as she thought about it, she realized there was a way out of her predicament. Mr. Hopper had not left town yet. She could still deliver the money to him early tomorrow morning.

"Mr. Roberts?" she called. He was making his way slowly toward his house.

He turned and smiled. "Yes, dear?"

Jessica ran toward him. "Do you know what time Mr. Hopper's planning to leave tomorrow?"

"Jim said he wanted to get an early start. Around six in the morning."

"Thank you, sir," Jessica said. She headed back down the street. She would have to get up first thing in the morning, on a Saturday. Still, it was the only way to get out of this mess without her father ever having to know about it.

Jessica clutched the envelope nervously. Five hundred dollars was a huge amount of money. What could she do with it overnight? She had to be absolutely certain that it wouldn't get lost.

She smiled to herself as she turned the corner toward home. It was simple enough. She would just hide it in an extra-safe place where nobody would ever look. Jessica knew she would find the perfect spot. She just had to concentrate.

What she needed was a place where no one would be likely to go that evening. Not Steven, or Elizabeth, or her father. A room nobody used.

Suddenly she had an idea: The utility closet! It was the place where her mother stored all kinds of odds and ends such as the vacuum cleaner, Steven's baseball equipment, and other assorted junk. The perfect hiding place!

Jessica tiptoed into the house with the envelope safely hidden under her shirt. She walked directly to the utility closet, opened the door, and quickly unzipped the cover on the tennis racket that was lying on the top shelf. The cover had a side pocket for holding tennis balls, and it was just the right size for hiding five hundred dollars.

Jessica stood on her tiptoes and slipped the case off the racket. Steven hadn't used it in months. She thought maybe it belonged to one of his friends, but it had been stashed in the closet so long that it was hard for her to remember. In any case, knowing Steven, the racket would sit there forever.

She had just unzipped the side pocket when

she heard a noise at the far end of the hallway. It was Steven. He had his nose buried in the TV schedule, and was heading for the den.

With lightning-quick speed, Jessica stuffed the envelope into the tennis racket pocket. She put the racket back into the case, threw it onto the top shelf, and closed the closet door. Then she leaned against the wall as casually as she could, crossing her arms over her chest.

As Steven passed by, she smiled sweetly. He glanced up from his magazine. "What are you doing, Jess?" he asked. "Holding up the wall?"

"Very funny, Steven," she responded. "You're such a comedian."

Jessica waited until Steven was out of sight. Her heart was racing and her palms were damp, but she had accomplished her mission. She breathed a long sigh of relief. The money would be safe until tomorrow morning.

Three

◇

Jessica found Steven glued to the TV set a few minutes later.

"Where's Elizabeth?" she asked.

Steven shrugged. "I think she's upstairs reading. I guess she doesn't appreciate my good taste in television shows."

Jessica giggled. "Aren't you a little old to be watching cartoons?" she asked.

"Actually, this is very educational," Steven responded with a grin.

Jessica grinned back. "Yeah, I guess cartoons are right at your intellectual level. You wouldn't want to strain your brain."

Steven playfully tossed one of the couch pillows in Jessica's direction. Then he turned his attention back to the television. Jessica felt assured that Steven didn't suspect a thing.

Just then Mr. Wakefield strode purposefully into the den. "Dinnertime, troops!" he announced. He scanned the room, looking annoyed. "Pick up those newspapers, will you?" he said to no one in particular. "And where's Elizabeth?" he added.

Before Jessica or Steven could answer, their father disappeared into the kitchen. Steven turned off the television. He and Jessica arranged the scattered newspapers into a neat pile.

"Watch out," Steven whispered. "I think Dad's going through one of his cleaning phases."

"Uh-oh." Jessica wrinkled her nose. "The last time he did this, we had to clean every square inch of our bedrooms. It took me an entire weekend!"

"Well, whatever you do, don't complain," Steven advised her. "Dad's been working awfully hard on that new case. He hasn't been in a very good mood lately."

"I noticed." Jessica nodded. "I've already gotten into trouble once today."

"You?" Steven pretended to be surprised. "Saint Jessica?"

He ran toward the kitchen before she could swat him with a newspaper. Jessica followed behind, grumbling at Steven under her breath.

Mr. Wakefield was in the kitchen, busily rearranging the dishes in the cupboard. "Sorry, kids. False alarm," he told them. "Guess I called you too soon. The roast needs a few more minutes." He turned to face them. "How about putting the time to good use? The house could use a good cleaning."

Steven gave Jessica an I-told-you-so look.

Mr. Wakefield rubbed his hands together. "Steven, you take the den," he said. "And Jessica, the upstairs hallway needs to be vacuumed. If you can't get it all done before dinner, you can finish later."

"I'll take care of it, Dad," Jessica said, turning to leave. She was eager to stay out of his way. There was no telling what other chores he might come up with.

"Not so fast, young lady," Mr. Wakefield said. "You're not getting off that easily. I'd also like all the towels in the dryer folded and put into the bathrooms," Mr. Wakefield added.

"OK," Jessica said meekly. "Is that all?"

"Isn't that enough?" her father asked with a grin.

"Plenty!" she answered, returning his smile.

Jessica headed upstairs to Elizabeth's room. She found her twin lying on her bed, reading a mystery novel. The radio was playing quietly.

"Where have you been?" Elizabeth asked curiously.

"Downstairs, getting chores dumped on me," Jessica said unhappily. "Dad's turning into Mr. Clean."

"No, I mean where were you earlier?" Elizabeth asked.

"Oh, running an errand for Dad," Jessica said. She sat down at her sister's desk. She hoped Elizabeth wouldn't ask for any details.

"What kind of errand?" Elizabeth inquired.

"No big deal," Jessica said quickly. "I just had to run a package down the street." She could feel her cheeks growing hot.

"I ran into Caroline Pearce," she announced, trying desperately to change the subject. "And you'll never believe what she told me!"

"I won't believe it because it's probably not true," Elizabeth responded.

Jessica laughed. "Caroline swears Bruce Patman is bringing a *date* roller-skating tonight. But she doesn't know who."

"Well, whoever she is, she has my sympathy," Elizabeth said. She thought Bruce was obnoxious and a bit of a bully.

Jessica ignored her twin's comment. "I just can't wait to see who it is," she mused. She picked up a pen from Elizabeth's desk and began doodling on a piece of notebook paper.

Elizabeth turned on her side and examined her sister carefully. "What time are you going roller-skating, anyway?"

"Right after dinner," Jessica answered. She was busy drawing little hearts with "Jessica + ?" written inside of them. "Ellen Riteman's mom is picking me up."

"How are you going to clear the table if you go roller-skating right after dinner?" Elizabeth demanded. "Remember our deal for the next three nights?"

"Oops," Jessica said uncomfortably. "I meant, starting *tomorrow* night." She gave Elizabeth an angelic smile. "Besides, that's the least of our problems. Dad wants the upstairs hall vacuumed *and* the towels in the dryer folded and put away."

"So?" Elizabeth asked, picking up her book. "I'll vacuum and you can do the towels."

"But I have to finish getting ready for tonight," Jessica moaned.

Elizabeth refused to take her twin's hint. She was tired of doing Jessica's share of the housework. "Then *you* can vacuum and *I'll* do the towels," she suggested.

Jessica frowned. She could tell she was getting nowhere with Elizabeth. It seemed like a good time to change the subject. "So, by the way," Jessica said, "what was the assignment Mrs. Arnette told us about in social studies class?"

"You were there, Jessica. Didn't you hear?" Elizabeth asked.

"Well, I was talking to Ellen." Jessica grinned sheepishly. "So I didn't quite hear everything."

"She said she's going to give us something big to do on Monday," Elizabeth explained. "She didn't give us any of the details. She just hinted that we should be prepared for something different and challenging."

"Oh, no," Jessica moaned. "That means something really hard. Like reading a whole long book or something."

"I don't think that would exactly kill you, Jess," Elizabeth said.

"Of course you don't," Jessica replied. "*You* love to read." She eyed the book in Elizabeth's hand. "So, speaking of books, what's that one about?"

Elizabeth knew Jessica was just trying to avoid the topic of the housework they were supposed to be doing. Jessica was never interested in the books Elizabeth read.

"It's the latest Amanda Howard mystery," Elizabeth said. "I've only read the first two chapters, but so far, it's wonderful."

Jessica made a face. "I just can't understand why you read books when they're not even homework."

"Well, I know you'll find this hard to believe," Elizabeth said, "but it's fun. I like to try to solve the mysteries." She got a dreamy look in her eyes. "Someday I might even write a book myself."

Jessica smiled mischievously. "I guess you'd expect me to read it, huh?"

"You're my sister," Elizabeth reminded her. "Of course I would."

Jessica nodded. "For you I'd even read a whole book. But personally, I'd rather watch TV or listen to music." She turned up Elizabeth's radio. A new song that she liked was playing.

"Have you heard this?" she asked, moving to the beat.

Elizabeth shook her head. "No, but I like it."

Jessica returned to her doodling. "So, anyway, about that stuff Dad asked us to do," she began. "I thought maybe we could flip a coin, or—" She stopped in the middle of her sentence and held up her index finger. "Wait a minute," she whispered excitedly. "Listen!"

The song had ended and the deejay was speaking. "This is it!" he said in a very deep, fast voice. "The all-new, all-time-best contest we at KSVR have ever put together for you, our rockin' listeners. That's right! It's our Name That Song Contest, and you, yes *you*, can win a cool thousand bucks by keeping your dial tuned to KSVR!"

"A thousand dollars!" Jessica repeated in awe.

"That's an awful lot of money," Elizabeth mused.

The twins sat in silence as the announcer explained the contest rules. All you had to do was send in your name and the name of your favorite rock star to the station, then stay tuned between four and nine P.M. every day. When one of the deejays came on and announced your name, you had five minutes to call the radio station. If you called within five minutes, the announcer would play a tape of five songs by your favorite singer. And if you could name all the songs, you'd win. There was only one catch: They would only play a few seconds of each song, so you really had to know the songs well. If you did, you could win a thousand dollars!

As the deejay finished explaining the contest, Jessica wrote the station's address on a piece of paper. She turned down the volume and smiled triumphantly. "Elizabeth, I just *have* to enter this contest! I know every song Johnny Buck ever sang. I know I could win!"

"But just by listening to a few seconds of each song? I don't know, Jess. That's not very much time. Besides, what if they don't call you? I bet lots of people will enter," Elizabeth said.

Jessica shook her head. "Look at what great luck we've already had with radio contests. Remember the time I won those tickets to the Melody Power concert? And how about the time you won that big party at Club Jupiter for naming that new radio show?"

"I wonder if we haven't just about used up our luck with contests," Elizabeth mused.

"I am a *very* lucky person." Jessica laughed. "Just think of what I could do with a thousand dollars! I could buy every outfit I ever wanted from Kendell's. Or maybe get my own TV set for my room. Or better yet, my very own telephone!"

"Or you could save the money for something important, like a trip, or maybe college," Elizabeth offered.

Jessica smiled. "Oh, Elizabeth, you're so *practical*." She reached for a sheet of paper. "Do you have any envelopes? I want to send in my entry right away."

"What about the chores?" Elizabeth wanted to know.

"First things first, Lizzie," Jessica said sternly.

The next morning, Jessica heard another announcement about the radio contest. Only this time it was on the clock radio in her room. And this time it was playing at five-fifteen in the morning.

Jessica took one look at the time and groaned. She turned off the radio and put her pillow over her head. She tried to think of one good reason for getting up at this hour. Then she remembered the angry look on her father's face yesterday afternoon. And her D in history. And her marathon phone conversation with Lila.

"OK," she grumbled aloud. "I'm coming." Jessica rolled out of bed. After glancing in her closet, she decided to wear a pair of white shorts with a red T-shirt.

While she dressed, she thought about the fun she'd had at the skating rink the night before. All the Unicorns had been there. For most of the evening, they had skated in a big group, holding hands as they circled the rink. Jessica was very proud of the fact that she had only fallen twice.

But as usual, Caroline Pearce had her gossip wrong. Bruce Patman *had* shown up at the rink, but he had come with two other seventh-grade boys. They spent the night wildly skating around the rink very fast. Now, as Jessica thought about it, she was sorry she had ever stopped to listen to Caroline Pearce. In fact, it was Caroline's fault that she had to get up so early.

Quietly Jessica went into the bathroom. Elizabeth's bedroom also connected with the bathroom, so Jessica tried to be quiet. She did not want Elizabeth waking up and asking a lot of questions. It took Jessica a few minutes to find the toothpaste, but she finally located it under a mound of dirty towels. Maybe Elizabeth had a point about cleaning up in there.

After she brushed her teeth, Jessica tiptoed downstairs to the kitchen. The house was completely quiet. Outside, the sun was just beginning to rise, and the sky was pale pink.

She headed for the utility closet and swung open the door. She could just reach the top shelf where she had placed the racket the day before. Jessica ran her hand along the shelf, but all she found was her mother's sewing basket.

That's strange, she thought. Jessica flicked on the closet light and peered inside. She could have sworn that the closet looked neater this morning than it had the day before. Anxiously she checked the other shelves. No racket.

Jessica ran back to the kitchen and pulled a chair away from the breakfast table. She dragged it through the hallway to the closet. The racket was probably way back on the top shelf. But, when she climbed up on the chair and searched the shelf, she found nothing there.

"Oh, no," she whispered, panic-stricken. "The racket is gone!"

Four

◇

Jessica stood frozen on the chair. Five hundred dollars, vanished, and it was *her* fault!

She pictured her father's face when she told him the horrible news. Her mind was filled with thoughts of all kinds of punishments awaiting her. She would never get an allowance again, ever. She would have to do all Elizabeth's and Steven's chores, in addition to her own. Maybe she really *would* be grounded forever. She would have to drop out of the Unicorns and live like a hermit. . . .

Jessica started to feel dizzy. She climbed down off the chair. *Stay calm,* she ordered herself, although she knew it was useless.

She still had one shred of hope, however.

Maybe the racket had been moved to some other part of the house. Maybe it wasn't lost, after all.

First, she would calmly search every nook and cranny of the house. *That* would be the kind of sensible, logical plan that Elizabeth always came up with in moments of crisis.

And if she still couldn't find the racket, *then* she would panic.

Jessica searched everywhere. In a corner on the floor she found a purple bracelet that she had lost months ago. But no racket. And that meant no money. And that meant she was in very serious trouble.

No doubt about it, it was definitely time to panic!

Jessica dragged the chair back to the kitchen and debated about what to do next. The most obvious thing was to ask Steven. It was *his* racket. He must have moved it last night. In all likelihood, it was probably in his bedroom right now.

Jessica dashed up the stairway to Steven's room. His door was closed. She stared at the NO TRESPASSING sign on his door and suddenly remembered what time it was. Steven loved to sleep, and he always tried to sleep until noon on Saturday.

"Well, not *this* Saturday," Jessica muttered under her breath. She began knocking on Steven's door, loud enough to wake Steven, she hoped, without awakening everyone else in the house.

She paused and put her ear to the door. All she heard was a loud snore.

"Steven!" Jessica hissed. "Wake up!" She pounded on his door again, a little louder this time.

After a few seconds she heard a muffled groan. "Go away!" Steven said.

Jessica opened her brother's door just a crack and looked inside. He was curled up in bed with the covers pulled over his head.

Jessica entered Steven's room and stepped quietly over a pile of baseball equipment and an assortment of clothing. She glanced around, but with the shades drawn, it was hard to see. She had no choice but to try to wake him up.

Jessica lightly touched Steven on the shoulder.

"Steven," she whispered loudly, "are you asleep?"

"Yes," he growled.

Jessica shook him again. "You are not!"

"I'm talking in my sleep," Steven responded in a muffled voice.

"Good. Then you can answer this question," Jessica said with determination. "What happened to that tennis racket that was in the utility closet?"

She waited impatiently for her brother's reply. After a long time, he answered with a quiet snore.

"Steven!" Jessica wailed. She plopped down at the foot of his bed and began bouncing up and down. Her life was falling apart, and her big brother couldn't even stay awake long enough to answer one simple question!

At last Steven emerged from underneath his quilt. He squinted at Jessica. His hair was tousled and he looked very confused.

"Just tell me one thing," he said groggily. "I *am* dreaming, aren't I?"

Jessica stopped bouncing and stomped over to the head of Steven's bed. She put her hands on her hips and said in her most no-nonsense voice, "Steven, will you *please* be serious?"

"It's worse than I thought," he moaned, closing his eyes. "I'm having a nightmare!"

That was more than Jessica could stand. She grabbed his pillow and began swatting him with it. "Wake up!" she cried. "Right now! Will you *please* tell me what happened to the tennis racket?"

"OK, OK. The racket," Steven repeated. "While Dad was on his cleaning kick last night, I guess he opened the utility closet and the racket fell on his head."

There, Jessica thought. Now she was getting somewhere. "So where'd you put it?" she asked eagerly. She scanned his bedroom. "I don't see it."

"That's because it wasn't mine. I borrowed it from Peter Moore a long time ago," Steven explained. He rolled onto his side. "Now give me my pillow."

"I'll give it to you, all right!" Jessica cried, whacking him again with the pillow. "Where is the racket now?" She had a terrible feeling she wasn't going to like his answer.

"I took it over to Peter's house last night," he told her, and then yawned widely.

"Oh, Steven, how *could* you?" Jessica groaned.

"What's the big deal?"

"Oh, nothing," she answered grimly. "It's just that my life is over."

"Well, as long as it's nothing serious," her brother said. "Can I have my pillow back now?"

Jessica tossed the pillow at him and turned to leave. By the time she reached the door, he was already snoring.

Jessica stepped out into the hallway, wondering why this was happening to her. She had to get that racket! But how was she going to explain to Peter why she wanted it? And what if he had already found the money? She needed help, and she needed it right away.

Elizabeth!

Jessica ran to her twin's bedroom door and knocked softly. "Elizabeth?" she whispered, opening the door and stepping inside.

Elizabeth was still asleep.

"Lizzie?" Jessica said.

Elizabeth rolled over and rubbed her eyes. "Jessica?" she asked. She checked her clock. "Do you know what time it is?"

Jessica sat down on the bed next to her sister. "I know, Elizabeth. But I need to talk to you this very instant."

"What's wrong?" Elizabeth asked. She sounded concerned.

Jessica took a deep breath. "See, it all started when I got that D in history and Dad was kind of mad at me and I wanted him to trust me. So he gave me five hundred dollars to give to Mr. Hopper, but then Caroline Pearce had to tell me some gossip about Bruce Patman, so I ended up putting the money in Peter Moore's tennis racket cover and now it's gone and, oh, Lizzie, what am I ever going to do?" Jessica fell back onto the bed dramatically and landed on Elizabeth's toes.

"Whoa!" Elizabeth exclaimed. She propped

herself up on her elbows and wriggled her feet free. "I only understood about half of that. Did you say something about five hundred dollars?"

Jessica nodded glumly.

"Now, tell me again," Elizabeth instructed patiently. "Only this time *slowly!*" She could tell from her twin's anxious expression that this was serious.

Jessica took a deep breath. She tried to explain the whole story more calmly. When she had finished, she looked over at Elizabeth to see what her sister's reaction would be.

"Well," Elizabeth said at last, "it seems to me that the most important thing right now is getting the money back. It's too late to worry about Mr. Hopper."

"But, Lizzie!" Jessica wailed.

"By the time we get the money, he'll already have left for his vacation," Elizabeth continued logically. "But we can give him the money when he gets back next week."

Jessica sat up. "I suppose you're right. And there's no reason Dad would ever have to find out what happened." Her eyes grew cloudy. "But first I have to get the money back, Lizzie! We've got to get over to Peter Moore's house!"

Jessica jumped off the bed and rushed over to Elizabeth's closet. "Here," Jessica said, grabbing a pair of shorts and a blue T-shirt and tossing them to her sister. "Get dressed and we'll ride over right now!"

"Wait a second!" Elizabeth said with a laugh. "It's way too early to go over to the Moores'. Besides, I'm sure the money's still in the ball pocket. And even if Peter found the money, it's not as if he'd keep it."

Jessica brightened. Elizabeth was so sensible. "You know, you're right, Elizabeth," she said, suddenly feeling much better. "Peter would immediately figure out that the money belonged to us."

Elizabeth snuggled back onto her pillow. "Don't worry, Jess. There won't be any problem," she reassured her sister. She yawned and closed her eyes.

"Hey, sleepyhead!" Jessica called. "How about if I make you a nice big bowl of cereal?" She was wide-awake and felt like having some company.

Elizabeth opened one eye. "I don't know, Jess," she responded. "Didn't you flunk cereal preparation in cooking class?"

Jessica laughed and headed for the door. "Breakfast will be served in five minutes," she announced. "And no more smart remarks about my cooking ability," she added, "or I'll do something *really* dangerous, like try to scramble eggs!"

Jessica skipped down the stairs, feeling wonderful. It was hard to remember why she had been so upset. As usual, Elizabeth was right. In a couple of hours, she'd have the five hundred dollars back, and life would return to normal.

Jessica prepared cereal and orange juice for Elizabeth and herself.

A few minutes later, Elizabeth came downstairs, still looking groggy. She and Jessica sat down to eat.

"My compliments to the chef," Elizabeth remarked when she'd finished. "That was the best bowl of cornflakes I've ever had."

"I *told* you I could cook!" Jessica replied with a smile.

Just then Mr. Wakefield came into the kitchen. "Good morning, early risers," he said with surprise. "Why are you two out of bed at this hour?" He walked over to the counter and began making coffee.

"Well . . ." Jessica hesitated. "We . . ."

"We're going bike riding," Elizabeth offered.

"That sounds like fun," Mr. Wakefield commented as he poured water into the coffee maker. "But why so early?"

"Because it's so nice and cool this time of day," Jessica responded quickly.

"Yes, it is." Their father gave them a disapproving look. "It's also a good time to catch up on work you haven't done, such as folding the towels. I see the hall was vacuumed, but one of you overlooked the rest of the work."

Jessica gulped. "I'll do it right now!" She stood up and ran for the basement.

"What's gotten into her?" Mr. Wakefield wondered aloud.

"Oh, you know Jessica," Elizabeth said. "Always in a hurry to help!"

Jessica finished the towels in record time. As soon as she was done, the twins jumped on their bikes and sped off in the direction of the Moores' house.

The Moores lived down the street from Ellen Riteman, in an old house with a big front porch. Jessica was already ringing the doorbell by the time Elizabeth joined her on the porch.

Peter answered the door. He was about Steven's height, with dark brown hair and a broad smile. He recognized the twins immediately.

"Gee, for a minute there I thought I was seeing double," he said with a laugh. "You're Steven Wakefield's sisters, right?"

Jessica stepped forward. "I'm Jessica, and this is Elizabeth," she said.

"Yeah, I've seen you two at our basketball games," Peter explained. "You're kind of hard to miss, if you know what I mean."

"You should have seen us back when we used to dress exactly alike!" Elizabeth told him.

Jessica tapped her foot impatiently. She was not there to chat. "Peter, we're here about that tennis racket you loaned to Steven," she said in a businesslike voice.

"The one he returned last night?" Peter asked.

"Yeah." Jessica nodded. She had decided it would be better not to explain the long story about the five hundred dollars. If Peter had found the money, he would mention it. If not, the fewer people who knew the truth about this mess, the better. "I was wondering if we could borrow the racket again, just for a little while?" Jessica asked, giving Peter her sweetest smile.

"That sure is a popular racket," Peter remarked, looking amused.

"It really *is* a nice tennis racket," Elizabeth pointed out.

"We'd only need it for a few minutes," Jessica said.

"A few minutes?" Peter chuckled. "That would be an awfully quick game of tennis."

"Jessica meant a few *hours*," Elizabeth corrected her sister hastily. She gave her twin a sly grin. "You're not going to beat me *that* quickly, Jessica," she added, winking at her twin.

"Well, I'd like to help you out, but that racket belongs to my father," Peter told them.

"Your father?" Jessica repeated faintly.

"And it's a good thing Steven returned it when he did, because my dad needed the racket to play tennis with an important business client this morning. In fact, they're out playing now."

"You mean he's using the tennis racket right this minute?" Jessica blurted out. She was panic-stricken for the second time that morning.

Peter nodded. "My dad plays tennis with clients every now and then. Usually he lets them win," he said with a smile. He studied Jessica sympathetically. "Hold on. I've got an idea." Peter disappeared from view.

"Now what do we do?" Jessica whispered.

Elizabeth shrugged helplessly. "I'm not sure," she answered.

Peter reappeared at the door. He was carrying

another tennis racket. "Here," he said to Jessica. "Be my guest." He handed her the racket. "This is my mom's, but she never plays tennis anymore. You can borrow it for as long as you like."

Jessica stared blankly at the racket in her hand. "But this isn't what . . ." she began, her voice trailing off. "Thanks," she finished lamely.

"Anytime," Peter answered cheerily. "And good luck with your game!"

He closed the door, and the twins walked slowly toward their bikes.

Elizabeth glanced at her sister. She hated to say what she was thinking, but she couldn't think of an alternative. "Well, I guess the only thing you can do is tell Dad what happened," she said, trying to sound cheerful. "Hopefully we can get the money back later today."

But Jessica wasn't ready to give up. "Not yet, Elizabeth," she said with determination. "I don't care what it takes. I'm going to find that money, even if it's the last thing I do!"

"But how?"

"Simple," Jessica answered confidently. "We'll just go from tennis court to tennis court until we find Mr. Moore. Then I'll go up to him and ask very politely if he's seen five hundred dollars lying around anywhere." She paused. Elizabeth was shaking her head in a very discouraging way.

"Do you know how many tennis courts there are in Sweet Valley?" Elizabeth asked her.

"Ten?" Jessica ventured.

"More like a hundred. We'd be looking for days!"

Jessica threw back her shoulders and climbed onto her bike. "We've gotten out of worse messes than this," she said. "That money is out there somewhere, Elizabeth, and I'm going to find it!"

Five

◇

Jessica and Elizabeth had only ridden a few blocks when they heard Caroline Pearce call out behind them. She was coming toward them on her bike. "Wait up, you guys!" she yelled.

The twins stopped by the side of the street. "Here we go again," Jessica whispered to her sister. "This whole mess started when I stopped to talk to Caroline. If it wasn't for her, Mr. Hopper would already have his five hundred dollars."

Caroline rode up next to them. "I'm so glad I caught up with you," she said breathlessly. "I can't wait to hear all about last night. Too bad about Lila."

"What *about* Lila?" Jessica demanded.

"About being knocked out when she skated into a wall," Caroline explained matter-of-factly.

"What?" Jessica cried. "Caroline, you've really gone overboard this time! Lila didn't get knocked out." She rolled her eyes.

"That's not what *I* heard," Caroline said defensively.

"Caroline, I was there. Trust me, you heard wrong," Jessica told her. "Can you believe that rumor, Lizzie?" she said, turning to her twin.

But Elizabeth wasn't listening. She had pulled Mrs. Moore's tennis racket out of Jessica's bicycle basket, and was examining it carefully.

Jessica turned her attention back to Caroline. "The *real* truth, Caroline, if you must know, is that Lila fell down a lot, but she never ran into a wall. And she was never knocked out." Jessica gave her a superior look. "So that's one rumor you can kill right here."

"Oh," Caroline muttered. "Well, I guess you cleared that up." For a second she looked vaguely disappointed, but then she brightened. "So what happened with Bruce Patman?"

"Well, he didn't bring a girl. You had that wrong, too," Jessica informed her. "Actually, I think he wanted to skate with me during the couples skate, except that . . . Ouch!" Jessica screamed when she felt Elizabeth's elbow dig into her ribs.

"What was that for?" Jessica asked, giving her sister a quizzical look.

"We've got to go," Elizabeth said innocently.

"Go where?" Caroline asked, being nosy as usual.

"Um, go to play tennis. We're going to play tennis," Elizabeth answered quickly.

"Yes, that's right," Jessica jumped in. "Our tennis game."

"You two are going to play tennis with only one racket?" Caroline demanded.

"We take turns with it," Jessica explained.

"Right," Caroline said suspiciously. "Well, all right, if you two don't want to tell me where you're going—"

"We're going to the Sweet Valley Country Club," Elizabeth said firmly.

"We are?" Jessica turned to face her twin.

Caroline was unconvinced. "Fine. See if I ever tell you anything again." She climbed on her bike and rode off.

"Caroline thinks I was lying, and I was really telling the truth," Elizabeth murmured.

"You were?" Jessica asked. "Why there?"

Elizabeth's eyes were glowing. "Well, in the

mysteries I read, the first thing you always do is look for clues. Even little things can lead you in the right direction."

"So?" Jessica asked impatiently. As far as she could see, the problem had to do with money, not mystery novels.

"So, look at the bottom of Mrs. Moore's racket!" her sister exclaimed.

Jessica peered at the racket. Sure enough, stamped on the bottom were four tiny letters: S.V.C.C.

"Sweet Valley Country Club!" Jessica cried. "Elizabeth, you're a genius! That's *got* to be where Mr. Moore is playing tennis."

"Let's hope so, anyway," Elizabeth said, crossing her fingers.

Jessica tossed the racket back into her bike basket. The twins took off in the direction of the country club, pedaling as fast as they could. Minutes later, they arrived at the entrance to the club.

After parking their bikes, Jessica grabbed Mrs. Moore's racket and pointed to the location of the tennis courts. There were a dozen courts, all of them in use.

"Wow," Elizabeth said under her breath. "There are so many courts. Do you see Mr. Moore anywhere?"

"No, but I'll recognize him when I see him," Jessica reassured her. "I met him at one of Steven's basketball games. You weren't there, but he was talking to Mom and Dad, and they introduced me to him."

The girls followed a sidewalk until they reached the courts. Each one had a high chain-link fence around it. There were lots of other people standing around and watching the games, so nobody seemed to notice Elizabeth and Jessica.

They had almost reached the last tennis court when Jessica caught sight of Mr. Moore. "There he is!" she said in a hushed voice. "On the right."

"Are you sure?" Elizabeth peered through the steel fence. She saw two men dressed in white shorts, running furiously back and forth across the court.

"Positive." Jessica nodded her head. "Now, follow me. And try to look casual."

Elizabeth walked with her twin toward the court, but she definitely was *not* feeling casual. They stopped behind a large tree. "What are you going to do?" Elizabeth asked. She was not in the mood for one of Jessica's schemes.

"See over there?" Jessica pointed to the edge of the court next to the fence. Near a pile of white towels, she could clearly see Mr. Moore's white tennis racket cover, the cover in which she had stashed the five hundred dollars. "That's the racket cover," Jessica told her sister. "And if I crawl through those bushes next to the fence, I might be able to reach it!"

"Jessica, no!" Elizabeth argued. "What if somebody sees you?"

"I'll be careful," Jessica reassured her. "I have to try, Elizabeth. I can't stand the suspense any longer!" She handed Elizabeth Mrs. Moore's racket.

Before Elizabeth could say another word, Jessica ran off. She headed for the thick bushes that grew next to the fence and began wriggling through them. The branches were very prickly, and Jessica wished she had worn jeans instead of shorts. Her legs were covered with scratches.

Through the bushes, Jessica could make out Mr. Moore serving the ball. She squeezed her hand through the fence. With her fingertips she could just barely touch the racket cover. Unfortunately, she couldn't quite grasp the zipper. Jessica tried to feel the pocket to see if the money was still inside. But it was hard to tell.

She made one last attempt to reach the zipper. Just when she was sure she had it, she felt the racket cover begin to move away from her. Jessica let out a squeal of surprise and yanked her hand back. Peering through the bushes, she could see that Mr. Moore and his client had finished playing and were reaching for their towels. Luckily, nobody had seen her.

Jessica looked back at Elizabeth. She was hiding behind the tree. She looked very nervous.

By the time Jessica managed to crawl out of the bushes, the two men had already left the court. Jessica brushed the leaves and dirt off her shorts and ran over to rejoin Elizabeth. "Where did they go?" Jessica asked desperately.

Elizabeth pointed down the sidewalk to a low wooden building marked MEN'S LOCKER ROOM.

"Quick!" Jessica said. "Let's follow them!"

Elizabeth grabbed her twin's arm. "Jessica," she said calmly. "You know I'd do almost anything to help you out of this. But I'm *not* going into the men's locker room."

Jessica smiled. She had to admit Elizabeth had a point. "All right. Let's just go and wait near the door."

The twins followed the sidewalk leading to the locker room. Outside the door was a long wooden bench.

"Was the money still in the pocket?" Elizabeth asked as they sat down.

"I don't know," Jessica said. "I could barely

reach it." She stared at the locker room door anxiously. "I hope they come out soon."

Elizabeth nodded her head in agreement.

They sat patiently for several more minutes, until Jessica couldn't stand it anymore. "Where *are* they?" she cried in frustration. "How long does it take for someone to shower?"

"According to Steven, it takes *you* about three hours," Elizabeth responded with a giggle. She stood up and gazed at the small building. "Do you think there's another door?"

Jessica shrugged.

"Watch this door," Elizabeth told her. "I'll be right back."

Elizabeth walked around to the side of the building. Just as she had guessed, there was another way out of the locker room. "Jessica!" she called. "Come here! There's a side exit!"

Jessica ran to join her sister. "They could be anywhere by now," she said. "Maybe Mr. Moore knew I was in the bushes all along, and he's trying to escape so he can keep the money for himself."

"Don't you think that's kind of unlikely?" Elizabeth asked.

"You always tell me that in your mystery novels, the bad guy is the person you least suspect," Jessica pointed out.

But Elizabeth didn't respond. She was walking quickly toward the main building where the club's restaurant was. "I think I saw him, Jess!" she yelled. "Come on!"

Together they ran up the steps to the front entrance of the restaurant. Over the door a big sign in green letters said THE CENTER COURT. A doorman dressed in a green uniform held the door open for them. "Wow," Jessica whispered, "this place sure is fancy."

The lobby was decorated with photographs of famous tennis players. As soon as they were inside, a pretty woman in a black dress approached them. She was carrying menus. "How many?" she asked with a smile.

"Two," Jessica answered automatically.

"Follow me, please," the woman said, heading toward the dining room.

"Jess!" Elizabeth hissed. "We can't go in there!"

"Of course we can. Lila does it all the time at her dad's country club."

"But Lila's father is a member!" Elizabeth argued. "She probably just charges everything to him." Elizabeth reached into her shorts pocket. "I have a grand total of ninety-five cents with me. How do you expect to pay for a meal? By doing the dishes?"

"We're not going to order anything, silly," Jessica answered. "I just want to see if Mr. Moore's in there. This way I can see without anyone asking me what I'm up to."

The hostess stopped and turned to face them. "Are you coming, ladies?" she asked politely.

Jessica strode forward confidently. "We're coming," she announced.

Elizabeth followed quietly. She had a funny feeling that Jessica had no idea what she was going to do next.

The hostess led them to a small round table covered with a green tablecloth. Jessica picked a chair and sat down. Elizabeth set Mrs. Moore's tennis racket on the floor.

"So, who won the game?" the hostess asked as she handed each girl a menu.

"Oh, um, I did," Jessica spoke up. "My sister's still a beginner."

"Well, enjoy your meal. The waiter will be right with you."

As the hostess walked away, Jessica giggled. "See, Lizzie? She thought we were playing tennis, so we fit right in. Now you can stop worrying." Jessica began glancing over the menu. "Mmm. Suddenly I'm starving."

Elizabeth yanked the menu from her sister's

hand. "We're not here to eat, Jessica. Hey, I see Mr. Moore," she whispered. "Over there by the window, sitting with his client. Whatever you're going to do, Jessica, you had better do it quickly. Our waiter will be here any minute!"

"All right! Just give me a second!" Jessica chewed on her bottom lip. One possibility was simply to walk over to Mr. Moore, introduce herself, and explain the whole crazy story. But that would be embarrassing, and Jessica hated to be embarrassed. Besides, there was a good chance Mr. Moore would go straight to her father and tell him what had happened.

When she looked over at Mr. Moore's table again, his client was still sitting there, but Mr. Moore had walked over to another booth. He was talking with two other men and laughing loudly.

Just then a busgirl arrived at the men's table. She was wearing white shorts and a green T-shirt, and carrying a large pitcher of ice water. While the twins watched, she picked up the empty glasses on their table and poured each of them a glass of water. When she finished, she walked over to a small work station in the corner of the dining room and set down the water pitcher.

"I've got it!" Jessica cried.

"What?" Elizabeth asked skeptically.

"Just watch," Jessica said. When the busgirl disappeared through a set of swinging doors, Jessica stood up. "If the waiter comes, tell him we haven't decided yet," she told Elizabeth.

Jessica confidently marched over to the area where the busgirl had left the pitcher. While Elizabeth watched in amazement, Jessica picked up the pitcher and headed toward Mr. Moore's table.

Jessica hoped everybody would think she was a real busgirl. After all, she had white shorts on, just like the other girl. And people sometimes told her that she looked older than her age.

Jessica glanced nervously to her right. Mr. Moore was still chatting at the other table. She looked to her left. Mr. Moore's client was sitting alone at their table, reading a newspaper. She could see Mr. Moore's tennis racket under the table, leaning against the wall.

Now was her big chance. Trying to look casual, Jessica approached the table.

"Hello," she said hoarsely.

"Hi," the man muttered, staring intently at his paper.

Jessica set the pitcher down on the table and reached for his empty glass with a trembling hand. While she steadied the glass with her left hand, she picked up the pitcher with her right. But she was so nervous that her arm began to shake and she overfilled the glass. Ice water gushed onto a section of newspaper lying on the table.

"Oh, I'm so sorry!" Jessica cried. She grabbed a napkin and began mopping up the pool of water.

The man picked up a corner of the newspaper, which was now a soggy mess. "Don't worry about it," he reassured her.

Jessica managed to smile. This busgirl stuff was harder than it looked. She glanced over her shoulder cautiously. Mr. Moore was still talking to his friends.

"I'm sort of new at this," she explained anxiously.

"I already read the sports section, anyway," the man said with a wink. He turned his attention to the rest of his paper.

Jessica knew it was time to put her plan into action. As she reached for the other water glass, she pretended to knock a fork to the floor accidentally. It bounced off of her foot and skidded to a stop.

"Oops," Jessica murmured. She knelt down on the floor and felt around for the fork. Mr. Moore's tennis racket was just within her reach.

At last! she thought with satisfaction, unzipping the cover pocket. She eased her hand inside, feeling for the envelope of money.

But there was nothing there! Absolutely nothing.

Jessica was horrified. She stayed down on the floor, wondering what to do next. Suddenly she felt someone standing over her.

"Looking for something?" came a solemn male voice.

Her heart racing, Jessica looked up to see Mr. Moore. He wasn't smiling.

Six

◇

Jessica sat on the floor, stunned into silence.

"That's our busgirl," Mr. Moore's client explained. "She was looking for a fork."

"I don't think that's *all* she was looking for," Mr. Moore said suspiciously. He knelt down next to Jessica. "Wait a minute. Don't I know you?" He broke into a smile. "You're Ned and Alice Wakefield's daughter. I remember meeting you at one of Peter's basketball games." He extended his hand to Jessica, and they both stood up. "Let's see . . . Jessica, isn't that your name?"

"Yes, sir," Jessica answered meekly. She could feel her cheeks growing as red as her shirt.

"Are you working here at the restaurant?" Mr. Moore asked.

"Well . . ." Jessica hesitated. "Not exactly."

Just then, Elizabeth rushed to her side. She was carrying Mrs. Moore's racket.

"My goodness," Mr. Moore laughed, looking back and forth between the two of them. "Two for the price of one! I didn't realize you had a twin!"

"I'm Elizabeth Wakefield," Elizabeth said. She cast a worried glance at Jessica.

"Twin busgirls!" Mr. Moore's client exclaimed. "How unusual."

"We're not really busgirls," Elizabeth explained.

"That explains why your sister gave my newspaper a bath," the man said with a chuckle.

"I thought you seemed a little young to be working here," Mr. Moore added. He gazed at Jessica more closely. "I don't suppose you'd mind my asking what you were doing down there with my tennis racket?" Before Jessica could think of an answer, Mr. Moore noticed the racket Elizabeth was carrying. "And while we're on the subject, isn't that my wife's racket?"

Elizabeth nodded. "Your son, Peter, lent it to us this morning."

"But what we really wanted was *your* racket," Jessica chimed in.

Mr. Moore scratched his head. "This story is getting stranger by the minute," he remarked with a wry grin. "Why don't you two girls have a seat, and we'll see if we can get this whole thing straightened out."

"Boy, I sure hope we can," Jessica said under her breath.

Mr. Moore gave her a confused look and held out a chair. "Please, have a seat," he said politely.

Mr. Moore's client offered Elizabeth a chair beside him. "My name is Mr. Brooks, by the way," he said.

"If you'd like, we could buy you a new newspaper, Mr. Brooks," Elizabeth offered.

"That's very kind of you, young lady, but it won't be necessary," he said.

"Now, why don't we start at the beginning?" Mr. Moore suggested. "Why is it that you wanted my tennis racket?"

Jessica picked up her napkin and played with the edge of it. She really did not want to tell Mr. Moore the whole story, but she had no choice.

Elizabeth answered for her. "It wasn't your racket that Jessica wanted. It was the five hundred dollars hidden in the pocket of it."

Mr. Moore looked completely puzzled. "Five hundred dollars?" he repeated.

Jessica's heart sank. What if Mr. Moore had no idea where the money was? *Then* what would she do? "You mean you haven't seen the envelope with the money in it?" she asked desperately.

"What money?" Mr. Moore asked. "What envelope?"

As calmly as she could, Jessica repeated the sad story of Mr. Hopper's missing charity money. "I was so sure it would still be in the racket cover pocket," she said glumly. "But now it's gone forever."

"Cheer up, young lady," Mr. Brooks said with a sympathetic smile. "These things have a way of working themselves out."

"I'm certain that if Peter had discovered the money when Steven returned the racket last night, he would have called your brother immediately," Mr. Moore assured them. "But as soon as I get home, I'll search the house. Maybe the envelope managed to fall out somehow and get lost."

"Thank you, Mr. Moore," Jessica said sadly. "I'd really appreciate it."

Elizabeth stood up. "Here." She handed Mr. Moore his wife's tennis racket. "It was very nice of Peter to lend this to us, but I guess we won't be needing it."

"Especially now," Jessica agreed as she rose slowly from her chair. "After we tell Dad about this, my tennis-playing days will be over." She sighed dramatically. "I'll probably never be let out of my bedroom again. Ever."

Mr. Moore couldn't resist laughing. "Speaking as a father with many years of experience, I think I can safely say you're overreacting just a bit. Of course your father will be upset, but I seriously doubt that you'll be spending the rest of your life in your room, Jessica."

Jessica forced herself to smile. "Thanks, Mr. Moore."

The twins waved goodbye and headed toward the exit.

"Wait a second, Elizabeth," Jessica said as they passed the table where the hostess had seated them. "Can I borrow your ninety-five cents?"

"I guess," Elizabeth said, reaching into her pocket. "What for?"

Jessica took the change and placed it on their table. "I know we didn't eat anything, but I want to leave a tip," she explained. "I never realized before how hard it is to work in a restaurant."

"I think I'll run away to the circus," Jessica announced when she and Elizabeth were a couple of blocks from home.

"Will you please be serious?" Elizabeth exclaimed. "We can figure out where the money is if you help me think about it logically."

"It's too late for logic," Jessica argued. Her long hair streamed behind her as she rode. "Now it's time to . . . to—"

"—to panic?" Elizabeth suggested. "Jessica, I'm sure there's an explanation here somewhere."

"Let's slow down," Jessica said. "We're almost home, and before I get there I want to decide what I'm going to do."

"Oh, all right," Elizabeth agreed. They slowed their bikes to a stop and began walking them. "Well, if you're going to join the circus, how about trying out as a clown first?" she suggested.

"Very funny, Elizabeth," Jessica pouted. "My life is ruined, and you're telling me I should be a clown."

"Well, you'd be a good clown. And, I want you to promise me that you'll send postcards from all the cities the circus stops in." Elizabeth laughed.

"You can laugh, but I'd rather run away than face Dad with this mess." Jessica shook her head. "Especially considering the mood he's been in."

"Well, I have to admit it would be nice not having to share the bathroom anymore," Elizabeth mused with a straight face. "But before you pack your bags, maybe you should try one last time to figure out what happened to the money."

"If you say so." Jessica shrugged. "I'll try, but I doubt it will help."

Just ahead of them, the Wakefields' home came into view. Steven was in the driveway. He was sitting cross-legged on the ground, trying to fix the chain on his ten-speed bicycle.

"Let's start with Steven," Elizabeth suggested. "Maybe he can give us some clues."

"I already talked to Steven," Jessica replied in a hopeless tone.

They turned into the driveway. "Yeah," Elizabeth said, "but Steven was just talking in his sleep this morning. Now he's actually awake."

Jessica glanced at Elizabeth. The last thing she wanted to do was to confide in Steven. If he knew she had lost five hundred dollars, he would make her life miserable. Steven would never let her live it down.

Elizabeth could tell what Jessica was thinking. "I don't think we have any choice, Jessica," she told her twin. She walked straight toward Steven. "Steven, do you promise that no matter what we tell you, you'll *never* breathe a word of it to anyone?"

Steven wiped his brow. "Wow, you guys must be in big trouble," he said seriously.

"Really big," Jessica said, sighing. "You know that tennis racket you borrowed from Peter?"

Steven nodded.

"Well, yesterday Dad asked me to deliver some money to Mr. Hopper's house. He lives over on Walnut Street. Anyway, I got kind of sidetracked and didn't get the money to him on time, so I decided to hide it overnight in the tennis racket cover."

"Uh-oh," Steven said. "I think I'm beginning to get the picture. You want me to call Peter?"

"We've already been to Peter's house," Elizabeth told him. "His father was playing tennis with the racket this morning. So we went to the club where his father was playing and checked the racket case, but the money was gone."

"You said 'some' money." Steven looked at Jessica. "How much is 'some'?"

"Five hundred dollars," Jessica whispered sullenly.

"FIVE HUNDRED DOLLARS!" Steven echoed, nearly screaming.

"Shh," Jessica cried. "Do you have to tell the whole neighborhood?"

"Sorry." Steven glanced around to see if his father was anywhere in sight. "Boy, you two weren't kidding. You *are* in big trouble." His face was grave.

Somehow, the fact that Steven wasn't teasing her about it made Jessica feel even worse. Even Steven thought this was serious!

"So, how can I help?" Steven asked.

"I thought maybe we could retrace your steps last night," Elizabeth suggested. "Maybe you'll remember something that would help."

"Let's see," Steven said thoughtfully. "Right before dinner, Dad asked me to clean the den. I was in there picking stuff up when he came in. He was rubbing his head. I guess he had opened the utility closet and the racket had fallen on him. He told me to return the racket to whoever it belonged to, and to clean the rest of my junk out of the closet."

"I *thought* it looked neater in there," Jessica said. "So you never saw the envelope with the money?"

"Never." Steven shook his head. "After dinner I rode my bike over to Peter's house and returned the racket." He gave Jessica an apologetic smile. "Sorry, Jess. But the money's bound to turn up, you know. It couldn't have just disappeared off the face of the earth."

"Thanks anyway, Steven," Jessica answered.

"Cheer up," Steven reassured her. "You'll find a way out of this mess."

"Now will you admit that I'm doomed?" Jessica demanded once she and Elizabeth were inside.

"Nope," Elizabeth said with determination. "Before we give up, I think we should search the house one last time. I'll take the utility closet. You take your room."

"My room?" Jessica echoed in surprise. "But it's such a . . . mess!"

"Exactly," Elizabeth said. "That's why it would be awfully easy for something to get lost in there. You could hide an elephant in your room and never find it again!"

"OK," Jessica said doubtfully. "I'll try anything!"

Jessica trudged upstairs, feeling completely defeated. When she got to her room, she turned on the radio, hoping it would make her feel better.

She began a halfhearted search through the clutter on her dresser. *This is pointless,* she thought to herself. *Wherever the missing money is, it isn't here.*

Just then the deejay on the radio announced the Name That Song Contest Jessica had entered the night before. "Boy, could I ever use a thousand dollars," she murmured out loud. "All my problems would be solved."

That was it! She didn't have to give up yet! All she had to do was come up with five hundred dollars before Mr. Hopper got back next week. It was *so* simple, it was brilliant!

Jessica rushed down to Elizabeth, taking the stairs two at a time. She found Elizabeth on her hands and knees, searching the bottom of the utility closet.

"Sorry, Jessica," Elizabeth said sadly. "I've searched everywhere. It's definitely not in here. Did you have any luck?"

"Yes," Jessica told her eagerly.

"You found the money?" Elizabeth cried, jumping to her feet.

"Well, I wasn't *that* lucky. But I did come up with a plan." Jessica looked over her shoulder. "Where's Dad?" she whispered.

"In his study," Elizabeth answered. "Why don't we go outside to the thinking seat? It's more private out there than it is in here."

The thinking seat was the limb of an enormous pine tree in the Wakefields' backyard. The twins used to play there for hours when they were younger. Elizabeth still loved to sit there to solve her problems or to read. Jessica claimed she had outgrown the thinking seat, but today she had to admit that it was the perfect place to reveal her plan.

"All I have to do is come up with five hundred dollars by next week," Jessica explained as soon as they were settled.

"Oh," Elizabeth groaned. "Is *that* all?"

"The radio contest, Lizzie! With a thousand dollars, even after I give half to Mr. Hopper, there'd be tons left over."

"But, Jessica, there's no guarantee you're going to win," Elizabeth said. She leaned back against the huge trunk of the pine tree. "Unless— Unless you could somehow manage to *earn* the money in a week," Elizabeth said.

"Earn it? Wouldn't it be easier just to win the contest?" Jessica said.

"Can you guarantee you'll win?" Elizabeth demanded.

"No," Jessica admitted reluctantly. "Maybe you're right."

"Of course, it's an awful lot of money," Elizabeth pointed out.

"But couldn't we do odd jobs around the neighborhood?" As far as Jessica was concerned anything would be better than telling her father the truth—even working! "I'm sure we could do it!"

"Wait a minute." Elizabeth's eyes narrowed. "Did you say 'we'?"

"Well, after all, Lizzie," Jessica said, "if you'd been home yesterday afternoon, you know Dad would have asked you to run to Mr. Hopper's house instead of me, and you wouldn't have stopped to talk to Caroline for so long. Then none of this would ever have happened."

"That is a really pathetic excuse, Jessica, but all right," Elizabeth relented. "I'll help." The truth was she couldn't stand to see Jessica in so much trouble.

"Elizabeth Wakefield," Jessica said with a grateful smile, "you're the best sister in the world!"

Seven

"They're going to be very colorful," Jessica explained to Elizabeth, who was sitting on Jessica's bed watching her work.

Jessica knew that if she and Elizabeth were going to get enough odd jobs to earn the five hundred dollars, they had to advertise, so she was making flyers to hand out in their neighborhood. She had already spent several hours at her desk, coming up with a design.

"I'm putting a rainbow at the top, and maybe some stars along the edges. Then I thought I'd sprinkle some gold glitter over each one." She held a sample up for Elizabeth to examine.

"It's beautiful," Elizabeth said. "How many of these are you planning to make?"

Jessica cupped her chin in her hand. "Well, I thought I'd pass them out all over the neighborhood. What do you think, Lizzie? Fifty?"

"That's an awful lot of work," Elizabeth said. "And we only have a week. Maybe you should make them simpler."

Jessica stared at her sample flyer. "I guess you're right. Maybe I'll leave off the glitter."

"What are they going to say?" Elizabeth asked.

"That's where you come in, big sister. I thought you could make up a catchy slogan. After all, you're the one who likes to write." Jessica extended the sample and a red Magic Marker to her sister. "You can put something right there in the middle, under the rainbow."

While Jessica continued her drawing, Elizabeth tried to think of just the right name for their new business.

"How about Helping Hands?" she suggested at last.

"I love it!" Jessica exclaimed. "It's perfect!" She stared off into space for a moment. "You know, maybe we should stay in business even after we earn back the five hundred dollars."

"Do you really want to do odd jobs after school every single day?" Elizabeth asked skeptically.

"Well, no," Jessica admitted. "But I thought

you and I could run the business, and hire other people to do the actual work."

"Let's see if we can manage to survive this week, before we go into business full time," Elizabeth suggested.

Elizabeth gazed at the empty space under the rainbow Jessica had drawn. "We do odd jobs" was the first idea she scribbled down, but she decided that was too boring.

At last she had an idea. "How about this?" she asked, handing the flyer back to Jessica.

Jessica studied the poem Elizabeth had jotted down on the flyer. It read:

> HELPING HANDS
> There's no odd job
> too big or small.
> We'll do it fast—
> and we'll do it all!

"Elizabeth, that's great!" Jessica said. "We're sure to get lots of work with these. Tomorrow after school we can hand them out."

"Maybe we should start our own advertising agency," Elizabeth joked.

By dinnertime the twins had completed almost fifty flyers. "Gosh, this is a lot more work than I thought it would be," Jessica complained. She rubbed her right arm. "My hand is killing me from all this drawing."

Just then there was a knock at the door. "Come in," Jessica called.

It was Mr. Wakefield. "Hi, girls," he said. "I wanted to let you know dinner will be a little late." He smiled sheepishly. "It seems your dear old dad forgot to turn on the oven."

Jessica and Elizabeth giggled. "I did that once in cooking class," Jessica admitted. "My brownies looked like mud pies, and I couldn't figure out why."

"Like father, like daughter." Mr. Wakefield shook his head. "I guess I've been a little distracted lately." He glanced over the pile of flyers on the floor near Jessica's feet. "What are you working on?" he asked. "An art project?"

"Not exactly," Elizabeth said. She handed him the flyer she had just completed.

"Helping Hands," Mr. Wakefield read aloud. He stroked his chin thoughtfully. "Impressive! This is a wonderful idea." He handed the flyer back to Elizabeth. "Just be sure it doesn't interfere with your school work."

"It won't, Dad," Elizabeth promised.

"And, by the way," he added as he turned to

leave, "I couldn't help noticing the state of your bathroom as I passed by just now. Before you start working for other people, why don't you give your own bathroom a helping hand?"

Elizabeth looked at Jessica. "Cross my heart, Dad," Jessica vowed sincerely. "By the time Mom gets back, that bathroom will be spotless."

"I knew I could count on you," he said. "And congratulations on your new business venture."

"Thanks, Dad," Jessica said with a guilty smile. *If only he knew the real reason we're going into business!* she thought to herself.

On Monday at school all Jessica could think about was the missing money. She got half the questions wrong on a pop quiz in math class because she couldn't concentrate. And she felt even more distracted during Mrs. Arnette's social studies class, especially since "The Hairnet" was going on and on about some boring new project. Mrs. Arnette had gotten her nickname because she always wore her hair in a bun neatly covered by a net. She was known for giving a lot of homework, and today would be no exception.

Jessica was amusing herself by making a list of the ways she would spend her thousand-dollar prize if she won the Name That Song Contest.

Five hundred dollars would have to go to Mr. Hopper, of course, but that still left five hundred dollars to spend just as she pleased.

At the top of her list Jessica wrote: "1. My own telephone. 2. TV set for my room." Every now and then she looked up and smiled vaguely at Mrs. Arnette, who was walking purposefully back and forth in front of the chalkboard as she explained the new assignment.

"This project is what is called a time utilization study," Mrs. Arnette said, reaching up to adjust her hairnet. "For one week, each of you will maintain a journal, keeping track of how you spend your time each day."

Jessica sighed and glanced across the room at her twin. Elizabeth was watching the Hairnet and smiling, as if she actually *liked* the idea of a week-long homework assignment.

"You'll need to note everything you do," Mrs. Arnette continued. "From eating to studying to watching television."

"Mrs. Arnette?" Winston Egbert said, shyly raising his hand.

"Yes, Winston?"

"You mean *everything*?" he asked. "Even, like, *sleeping*?"

"Everything." Mrs. Arnette nodded. "I think

you will be quite surprised at how your time is actually spent—and how much is wasted."

It's wasted on stupid assignments like this, Jessica thought sullenly. Mrs. Arnette began writing on the blackboard to show how she wanted the journals set up. As soon as her back was turned to the class, Jessica returned her attention to her list. "17." she wrote, "Silver earrings that I saw at Valley Fashions last week." Jessica was just about to jot down number eighteen when she heard Mrs. Arnette call her name.

"Jessica Wakefield," she said sternly as she turned around, "may I inquire as to exactly what you are doing?"

"I'm, uh . . . making a list," Jessica answered truthfully.

Mrs. Arnette smiled with satisfaction. "Well, naturally I'd prefer for you to wait until after school to get started on your assignment, but it's nice to see that you're taking such an interest." She marched over to Jessica's desk, arm extended. "Let's see what you have so far."

Jessica slumped down in her chair. Meekly she handed over her list.

For several agonizing seconds Mrs. Arnette contemplated the piece of paper, tapping her flat black shoe on the linoleum. Jessica chewed nervously on a fingernail.

"Well, it appears that you spend the greatest proportion of your time shopping, if this list is any indication," pronounced Mrs. Arnette. She passed the paper back to Jessica. "I'd suggest you spend a little more time on studying and a little less time at the mall, if you get my meaning."

"Sorry," Jessica mumbled.

Mrs. Arnette returned to the front of the class. "By the way, Jessica," she added, "how are you doing in math class these days?"

Jessica sneaked a questioning glance at Elizabeth, who shrugged helplessly. "OK, I guess," Jessica answered softly. "Why?"

"Because if my calculations are correct, buying everything on that list is going to cost you a small fortune." She gave Jessica a wry smile. "So, perhaps you should work on your arithmetic, too, dear."

"I can't believe the Hairnet gave us such a big project," Jessica moaned to Elizabeth in the gym locker room. "We've got enough to worry about this week, trying to earn back all that money."

Elizabeth knelt down to tie her running shoes. "I know," she agreed. "Still, don't you think it will be kind of interesting to see how we spend our time? I've never really thought about it before." She stood up and sprinted toward the door. "Come on, Jess. Gym class is being held out on the track today."

"I'm coming, I'm coming," Jessica said, frowning at her reflection. "I just want to put my hair in a ponytail."

Elizabeth laughed. "For example, have you ever thought about how much time you spend in front of the mirror?"

"I'll be sure to jot it down in my journal," Jessica answered, rolling her eyes.

Outside on the athletic field, Ms. Langberg, the twins' gym teacher, was already waiting on the grass at the edge of the gravel track. She gave a shrill blast on the silver whistle she always wore around her neck. "Let's go!" she yelled as the class straggled out the door from the gymnasium. "I don't have all day!"

"Today we are going to discuss the art of running," Ms. Langberg began when the class had assembled. A few of the girls snickered.

"For those of you who find that idea humorous," the teacher continued sternly, "I advise you to listen up. We're going to be running the hundred-yard dash today."

Elizabeth smiled. She liked to run. At the

other end of the line, Jessica was busy whispering with Lila and staring across the field at the boys' gym class.

"There's a lot more to sprinting than putting one foot in front of the other," Ms. Langberg explained. "A good start is crucial. Plus, you've got to pay attention to posture and arm movement. And, most importantly, you've got to learn how to breathe properly.

"If you practice all the things I've explained to you, I promise you'll run faster than you ever have before," Ms. Langberg finished several minutes later. "Now, let's see how well you were listening." She divided the class into groups of four. Jessica was in group one, Elizabeth in group two.

"Let's have all the 'ones' line up at the starting line," Ms. Langberg directed. Four girls, including Jessica, headed for the white line, where their teacher stood with the whistle in her mouth.

"Runners, on your marks, get set—" Ms. Langberg blew her whistle, and the four took off at high speed, heading for the finish line.

"Go, Jess!" Elizabeth called in encouragement.

But Belinda Layton, who was a very good athlete, finished several yards ahead of the others. Jessica came in a distant second.

"Group two, line up!" Ms. Langberg called.

"Good try, Jess," Elizabeth told her twin as they passed each other. She took her position with the other girls at the starting line, trying to remember all of Ms. Langberg's instructions.

When Ms. Langberg blew the whistle, Elizabeth took off in a flash. She moved her arms smoothly and kept track of her breathing, and, just as her teacher had predicted, she was able to move faster than she ever had before. To her amazement, she finished ahead of all the other runners!

After the other groups had run, Ms. Langberg asked the winners from each group to line up and race against one another. Once again, Elizabeth was off like a rocket. For the first half of the race she was in the lead, until Belinda Layton passed her in a sudden burst of speed, and won easily.

"Great race," Belinda told Elizabeth as they stood panting at the finish line.

"You know, I never realized how much there was to know about running," Elizabeth mused.

Before Belinda could answer, the boys' gym class raced across the far side of the field toward their locker room, whooping and hollering. One boy zoomed far ahead of the pack.

"Who's that?" Elizabeth asked in amazement.

"Danny Jackson," Belinda told her. "He's a great runner."

"Good enough to beat you?" Elizabeth teased.

"Definitely," Belinda answered, her dark brown eyes glittering.

"Good work, class!" Ms. Langberg called. "Hit the showers!"

As Elizabeth and Belinda headed toward the locker room, Jessica caught up with them. "That was some race, you guys," she told them. "Hey—" she paused suddenly. "Do you think we have to write down things like showering in our journals?"

"Sure," Elizabeth answered. "Like Mrs. Arnette told Winston, *everything* has to be included."

"Well, promise me one thing," Jessica said. "If it turns out I really *do* spend three hours a day in the shower, *don't* tell Steven, OK?"

Eight

◇

As soon as school ended, Elizabeth searched the halls, trying to find Jessica. She knew if they were going to get all the Helping Hands flyers distributed before dinner, they would have to hurry.

But Jessica was nowhere to be found. Elizabeth was about to give up when she ran into Amy Sutton near the front entrance to the school. Amy was dressed in her Boosters uniform and was carrying a baton. The Boosters was a cheering and baton squad the Unicorns had organized, and Amy was the only non-Unicorn member. They hadn't wanted to let her join until she proved to them that she was the best twirler in the middle school.

"What's wrong, Elizabeth?" Amy asked. "You look lost."

"*I'm* not lost, Jessica is," Elizabeth replied. Noticing Amy's uniform, though, she suddenly realized where her twin must be. "Wait a second. There's a track meet this afternoon, isn't there?" Jessica must have forgotten to mention it.

Amy nodded. "That's where I'm going now. Jessica's probably down at the track already. Want to come?"

"Sure," Elizabeth said. The truth was, she would much rather watch a track meet than wander around Sweet Valley passing out flyers.

Elizabeth and Amy headed for the track. It was a beautiful warm afternoon, and a small group of students and parents had already gathered in the stands. Jessica and the other Boosters were warming up, tossing their silver batons high into the air.

"You know, I've been to lots of basketball and football games, but hardly any track meets," Elizabeth said to Amy.

"They're really exciting," Amy told her. "The Boosters had a meeting and decided we have to support all school teams with equal spirit, so now we're cheering at every big track meet." She pointed across the field at a boy wearing gray sweat pants and a tank top. He was sitting on the grass, doing leg stretches. "Keep an eye on Danny Jackson. He sets a new record—"

"Elizabeth! Did you come to watch me cheer?" Jessica interrupted, running up to join them.

"I've seen you cheer a zillion times, Jessica," Elizabeth said, exchanging a smile with Amy. "Did you forget about Helping Hands?"

"Where's your school spirit, Lizzie?" Jessica demanded. "We can pass out flyers tomorrow."

"Flyers?" Amy inquired.

"Jessica and I are going into business," Elizabeth explained. She gave Amy a meaningful look. "It's a long story."

Amy smiled back. She had been best friends with Elizabeth long enough to sense that another problem was brewing.

Jessica glanced nervously at her watch. "It's almost four o'clock. Time for Name That Song." She ran over to her backpack near the foot of the stands and took her radio out. After clipping the radio to the waistband of her skirt, she put the earphones on and went to join Amy and Elizabeth.

"Jessica, you can't twirl a baton with earphones on!" Elizabeth exclaimed.

"What?" Jessica asked in a loud voice as she tuned in the radio. "I can't hear you."

Elizabeth reached over and gently pulled the earphones off. "I said, you can't cheer with those on."

"Sure I can," Jessica said with confidence.

"Why don't I listen to the radio for you during the meet?" Elizabeth suggested.

"No way," Jessica cried. "I want to hear my name announced to all of Sweet Valley."

"You entered that new contest on KSVR?" Amy asked.

Jessica nodded. "There's a thousand-dollar prize."

"Elizabeth's right," Amy warned Jessica. "You'll never be able to twirl with that on. Besides, chances are pretty slim that they'll call your name."

"You just wait," Jessica responded hotly. "I'm very lucky."

"Jessica! Amy! Hurry up!" Lila Fowler was waving at them impatiently. The other Boosters were already in line in front of the stands, ready to start the first cheer.

Elizabeth watched as Jessica and Amy ran to join the group. At the starting line, six runners had lined up for the first race, the hundred-yard dash. Elizabeth sat down in the first row of bleachers. From her seat she could see that Danny Jackson, the boy Amy had pointed out, was one of the runners.

"We are number one!" the Boosters yelled rhythmically. They tossed their batons into the air in perfect arcs. To Elizabeth's surprise, Jessica managed to catch her baton without any problem. Apparently the earphones weren't going to get in her way.

After the announcer at the top of the stands called out the runners' names, silence settled over the crowd. The runners took their positions. When the official's starting gun went off, the boys zoomed forward. Elizabeth watched Danny, trying to remember all the things Ms. Langberg had told them about posture, breathing control and arm movement. Danny ran effortlessly past the other runners and came bursting through the tape at the finish line.

"That's a new record for Sweet Valley Middle School, thanks to Danny Jackson!" said the announcer as the crowd applauded enthusiastically.

"Lean to the left, lean to the right; stand up, sit down, fight, fight, fight!"

The Boosters were doing another cheer. Elizabeth knew it was one of Jessica's favorites because she would get to be the center of attention at the end. While Amy and Ellen stood a few yards apart doing a complicated baton routine, the remaining six Boosters formed a pyramid: three girls on the bottom on their hands and knees; two kneeling on top of them; and *standing* on top of them, the last girl—Jessica.

The pyramid required very good balance, and the girls had practiced it for many hours to get it just right. To be on the safe side, they always performed the stunt on the grass field next to the track.

Today they were doing a perfect job. As Jessica climbed on top of the pyramid, she smiled radiantly. Once she had her balance, she threw her baton into the air, where it swirled in a silvery blur.

Everything was going perfectly until Jessica reached out to catch the baton. Her hand got caught on the wire connecting her earphones to her radio, and Jessica lurched forward to catch the falling baton.

Elizabeth watched in horror as Jessica's baton plopped to the grass, followed moments later by Jessica herself. The rest of the pyramid came tumbling down around her, in a tangle of arms and legs.

"Get off of me, you guys!" came Jessica's muffled cry from the bottom of the pile. "I'm suffocating!"

The Boosters untangled themselves, and clearly no one was hurt.

Jessica was the last to stand up. "Lila, I hate to break it to you, but you weigh a ton!" she said, brushing off her grass-stained skirt.

"Well, if you hadn't been wearing that stupid radio, none of this would have happened," Lila hissed.

While Lila and Jessica squabbled on the field, the announcer's voice came over the loudspeaker. "How about some applause for our fabulous Boosters? Don't worry, folks. It looks like everybody's fine."

Even though she wasn't hurt, Elizabeth suspected Jessica's ego was a little bruised. Today, at least, Jessica didn't seem to be lucky at all.

After school on Tuesday, Jessica and Elizabeth distributed their Helping Hands flyers around the neighborhood. At each house, they knocked on the door and handed out a flyer. If no one was home, they left a flyer in the mailbox.

It only took four blocks before they ran out of flyers. But to the twins' surprise, by then they had already lined up two jobs. Mrs. Etheridge wanted them to wash her car for five dollars. And Mr. Caldwell, who lived a few houses down the street from the twins, wanted his lawn mowed. He was willing to pay them ten dollars to do it.

"That's fifteen dollars!" Jessica exclaimed as they walked home. "At this rate we'll have the whole five hundred dollars in no time at all."

Elizabeth wasn't so sure. She was trying to figure out how long it would take them to wash a car *and* mow a lawn. "Do you think we can get all that work done after school tomorrow?" she asked anxiously.

"Of course," Jessica said confidently. "Don't forget, Elizabeth, 'There's no odd job too big or small. We'll do it *fast* and we'll do it all!' "

After her last class the next afternoon, Jessica caught up with Elizabeth in front of Elizabeth's locker.

"Hi, Jessica!" Elizabeth exclaimed as she closed her locker. "Are you ready for our first day of Helping Hands?"

Jessica did her very best to look disappointed. "You'll never believe this, Lizzie," she said as sadly as she could. "I was so excited about getting to work this afternoon, but now it turns out I have a Unicorn meeting right after school. Can you believe it? I'm so mad! But of course I have to go." She watched her sister carefully to see how she was reacting. Jessica had the uneasy feeling that Elizabeth wasn't falling for it.

"You're going to a Unicorn meeting? Do you think that you're going to eat cookies and watch soap operas while *I* do *your* work?" Elizabeth fumed. She lowered her voice to a whisper. "I didn't lose that five hundred dollars, Jessica Wakefield, *you* did."

"I know that," Jessica said defensively, staring down at the floor. "But you don't want me to be kicked out of the Unicorns, do you, Lizzie?"

"I don't think it would be the end of the world," Elizabeth said flatly. "Besides, they're not going to kick you out for missing one meeting."

"The Unicorns have very strict rules," Jessica reminded her twin.

"Well, so do I," Elizabeth answered firmly. "And if you're not going to help me, then there'll be only *two* Helping Hands instead of four! Your hands, Jessica!"

"OK," Jessica gave in. "I'm sorry. You go ahead to Mrs. Etheridge's house, and I'll be there as quickly as I can. I just have to stop by the meeting to explain why I can't stay."

Elizabeth glanced at her watch. "Well, you'd better hurry. It looks like it might rain."

"Don't worry, Elizabeth. After all, I *am* the president of Helping Hands."

"What does that make me?" Elizabeth asked.

"Vice-president, of course!" Jessica told her.

Elizabeth sighed. She was glad she didn't have to be vice-president for long.

Half an hour later, the vice-president of Helping Hands was cleaning out the inside of Mrs. Etheridge's blue Dodge. Elizabeth had just finished the upholstery when Jessica rushed up the driveway. "I'm sorry I'm late, Lizzie," Jessica said breathlessly.

"Good timing, Jess," Elizabeth said sarcastically. "I'm practically done with the inside!"

"I tried to hurry, Lizzie," Jessica protested. "Honest I did. But when I got to Janet's, there was this big argument going on, and naturally I had to stay and help settle things." She reached for Elizabeth's rag and began lightly scrubbing the steering wheel.

"I already cleaned that," Elizabeth said. "So, what was the fight about?"

Jessica stopped cleaning. "Well, believe it or not, Ellen Riteman actually wanted to change the official color of the Unicorns from purple to red." Each member of the Unicorn Club tried to wear something purple to school every day. Purple was their official color because it represented royalty.

"Ellen said she was tired of purple, and that kings and queens often wore red," Jessica continued. "We took a vote on it, and Ellen lost, of course."

"Well, that's a relief," Elizabeth teased. "What would you have done with all those purple clothes if Ellen had won?"

"Given them all to you," Jessica said lightly.

Elizabeth looked up at the sky. "It looks like it's going to rain any minute," she said. "And we still have to mow Mr. Caldwell's lawn." She looked at her watch. Then her eyes lit up. "I have an idea," she said. "How about if we split up? Since Mr. Caldwell has only one lawn mower anyway, it makes more sense for you to stay here and finish Mrs. Etheridge's car while I go start mowing."

"Good idea," Jessica agreed eagerly. She hated mowing lawns.

"All you have to do now is wash the outside," Elizabeth explained. "Mrs. Etheridge already gave me a pail of soapy water and a sponge. And the hose is right over there by the garage."

"I'll meet you back home when I finish," Jessica agreed.

Elizabeth walked to Mr. Caldwell's house as

fast as she could. He had a small lawn, but she was certain it was going to start raining soon. She wasn't sure she could finish mowing it in time.

When she arrived at his house, Mr. Caldwell showed her the shed where he kept his mower. Elizabeth groaned when she saw that it was an old-fashioned push-mower. Moving it across the grass took a lot of energy, especially since Mr. Caldwell's lawn was on a hill.

Elizabeth moved back and forth across the lawn as fast as she could. Her arms ached and her legs were sore, but she kept on going. Overhead the clouds had grown dark gray. Far off she could hear the distant rumble of thunder.

She was about to start on the backyard when she felt the first big drop of cool rain splatter on her arm. "Oh, no," she moaned. "Now I'll never finish."

Elizabeth returned the mower to the shed. Then she ran to Mr. Caldwell's front door. "It started raining," she explained apologetically. "But I could come back tomorrow afternoon to finish. Is that OK?"

Mr. Caldwell paid her for mowing half the lawn, and she agreed to come by right after school the next day to finish.

As Elizabeth ran home, it began to rain harder.

She stuffed the five-dollar bill from Mr. Caldwell into her jeans so it wouldn't get wet. Halfway home, Elizabeth realized there was no reason to hurry; she was already soaked. *I hope Jessica had better luck at Mrs. Etheridge's,* Elizabeth thought as she let herself in the back door. Then she sloshed upstairs to change her clothes.

Nine

◇

Jessica watched as soap suds slid down the side of the car. The rain was rinsing the car for her—all she had to do was watch!

Mrs. Etheridge leaned out of her front door. "Dear, wouldn't you like to come in the house until the rain dies down?" she called to Jessica.

"Oh, I don't mind," Jessica said with a laugh. "I'm already drenched anyway!" She held out her tongue to catch a raindrop.

"Oh, my," Mrs. Etheridge said as she adjusted her glasses. "Oh, dear me!"

"What's the matter?" Jessica asked.

"The windows!" Mrs. Etheridge exclaimed. "All the car windows are open!"

"Oh, no!" Jessica wailed. She closed the windows as fast as she could, but the front seats already looked like little wading pools.

Jessica walked very slowly through the pouring rain toward the house.

"I'm really sorry," Jessica told Mrs. Etheridge. "I completely forgot about the windows."

"Don't worry, dear," Mrs. Etheridge said kindly. "It's an old car. When the sun comes out again, we'll leave the windows open and it will dry in no time." She pressed a five-dollar bill into Jessica's palm.

Jessica thanked Mrs. Etheridge, gathered her backpack, and started home. *Only four hundred ninety-five dollars to go,* she thought glumly. She started to figure out how many more cars she would have to wash to earn the rest, but it was too scary to even think about.

"Look who's home—my sister, the drowned rat!" Steven greeted Jessica when she finally came into the Wakefields' kitchen.

Jessica set her wet backpack on the counter. She was too tired to argue with him.

"Guess what, Jessica?" Elizabeth exclaimed as

she joined them in the kitchen. "I have great news! Three more people called with odd jobs for Helping Hands!"

Just then Mr. Wakefield walked through the kitchen and noticed the puddle Jessica had made on the floor. He shook his head. "You know where the mop is, young lady!" he said cheerfully.

Jessica groaned. She felt like *she* was the one who needed a helping hand!

"Don't worry," Elizabeth told Jessica the next day, after school. "Today won't be nearly as bad as yesterday."

"How could it be any worse?" Jessica asked mournfully. She frowned as she examined her reflection in her full-length mirror. She was wearing her oldest pair of jeans and a purple T-shirt that had paint spots on it. Elizabeth had convinced her that there was no point in dressing up for their Helping Hands jobs. Jessica just hoped they wouldn't run into anyone from school while she was wearing such an ugly outfit.

"At least it's not raining," Elizabeth pointed out. "And as soon as I've finished mowing Mr. Caldwell's lawn, I'll come over and help you."

Jessica was going to start on the Helping Hands' next project: packing up boxes for a family that was moving. As bad as packing boxes sounded, she had to admit it was better than mowing lawns.

"I'm going to bring my radio with me and listen with my earphones," she told Elizabeth. "What if they call my name on KSVR for the contest, and I miss it because I'm doing some stupid job? All they have to do is pick me, and our troubles will be over!"

"You *do* have to answer their questions right first," Elizabeth reminded her.

Jessica gazed adoringly at the life-size poster of Johnny Buck hanging over her desk. "That's the *easy* part," she assured her sister. "Waiting for them to call is the hard part!"

When Jessica arrived at the Leaches' house, there were two cute little boys playing in the front yard.

"We're moving to Texas!" the oldest boy announced as Jessica approached. "They have real cowboys there."

"That's nice," Jessica said politely. "Is your mom home?"

"She's inside packing," the boy explained. "She hates to pack."

Jessica stepped cautiously inside the open front door. There were boxes everywhere. "Anybody home?" she called out.

"Oh, you must be from Helping Hands," said a pretty woman who was sitting on the floor, taping up a box. "I'm so glad you're here!"

"Where would you like me to start?" Jessica asked, trying to sound enthusiastic.

"Anywhere!" Mrs. Leach laughed, and then furrowed her brow in concentration. "Let's see. Upstairs in the first bedroom on the right there's a big pile of clothes I'm going to give away. You know, things the kids have outgrown or I don't want anymore. Why don't you start by folding those and putting them in one of these empty boxes?"

"Sure." Jessica smiled and reached for a big cardboard box. This was going to be easy!

"By the way," Mrs. Leach added, "I have a daughter who's in junior high school, and she's about your size. So if you see any clothes you'd like to keep, please feel free."

"Thanks," Jessica said in a doubtful tone. She started up the stairs to the bedroom.

The bedroom was practically empty, except for a bed with a huge pile of clothes on top of it. "Wow," Jessica murmured. It was bigger by far than the mountain of clothes on the floor of her own bedroom.

With her radio and earphones in position,

Jessica surveyed the pile. She halfheartedly folded a little boy's T-shirt as neatly as she could and laid it in the bottom of the box.

Sorting through the pile, Jessica was surprised to see a soft pink angora sweater with little pearl buttons down the front. She loved it, and it was just her size. She set it aside and began looking through the pile with more interest. Every time Jessica found something she especially liked, she tried it on over her own clothes to see if it fit.

Jessica spent the next hour making two piles: things she wanted to keep for herself, and everything else. She was almost at the bottom of the pile when she thought she heard Elizabeth talking to Mrs. Leach downstairs.

"Jessica?" Elizabeth called from the stairway. "Mrs. Leach wants us to help her pack up books in the living room. Are you almost done?"

Jessica glanced at the cardboard box. It was almost empty. "Um . . . almost," she replied breezily. "Can you come up here a minute, Elizabeth? I want to show you some things."

A few seconds later Elizabeth appeared in the doorway. Jessica took one look at her twin and gasped. Her face was dirty, bits of leaves were stuck in her ponytail, and she had grass stains on the knees of her pants. "What happened to you?" Jessica asked in amazement.

Elizabeth shrugged. "Mowing," she answered wearily. She studied Jessica more carefully. "What happened to *you*?"

Jessica spun around the room. "Do you like my new outfit?" she inquired.

"It's . . . um, unique." Elizabeth snickered.

Jessica was wearing the pink angora sweater over her purple T-shirt. She had a pink flowered skirt over her faded old jeans. And, on top of all that, she wore a bulky red bathrobe.

"Don't you think you're a little old to play dress-up?" Elizabeth asked.

"Mrs. Leach said I could have anything I wanted." Jessica decided to ignore her sister's sarcasm.

Elizabeth stepped forward and examined the empty cardboard box. "Jessica!" she gasped. "You've only folded one shirt in an hour?"

"Maybe you should take this bathrobe," Jessica said calmly. "It's more your style."

"One shirt!" Elizabeth marveled. "We could be here all night!"

"I never was very good at folding clothes," Jessica told her.

"Well then," Elizabeth said, turning to leave,

"this will be a wonderful chance to get some practice."

Before Jessica could reply, Elizabeth disappeared down the stairway.

Jessica stood in the empty room, staring blankly at the mound of clothing. As she picked up a pair of pants and began folding, the voice of KSVR's afternoon deejay caught her attention.

"Listen up, all you rockin' guys and gals!" he said smoothly. "It's time for another round of our Name That Song Contest, and some lucky listener could be one thousand dollars richer in a very few minutes!"

"Please," Jessica whispered. "Let him call my name!"

There was a long drum roll while the deejay picked out a postcard from one of the contest entrants. "Today's lucky lady is a big fan of the Dixon Brothers. Janice Taylor, I hope you're tuned in to KSVR, your all-hits all-the-time station. You've got five minutes to call us here at the studio. If you can name all five songs, you'll be our winner!"

When Janice Taylor did finally call in, she could only name one of the five songs the deejay played. Jessica realized that identifying a song could be difficult. Still, she was sure she could do it, if the songs were Johnny Buck's.

And the more clothes she folded, the more she was convinced that winning the radio contest was the only way out of this terrible mess.

That night, Elizabeth started to work on her journal for Mrs. Arnette's class. She sat on the couch in the den, her notebook in her lap, while Jessica sat on the floor thumbing through the newest issue of *SMASH!* magazine.

"You know, this is a lot more work than I thought it would be. You have to make a column for each activity, such as eating or watching TV," Elizabeth told Jessica as she drew neat lines on a piece of notebook paper.

"More work than packing books?" Jessica asked. She was not in the mood to worry about the Hairnet's latest annoying homework assignment.

"I've been taking notes on how I spend my time ever since Mrs. Arnette gave us that project to do," Elizabeth said. "How are you keeping track?"

Jessica sniffed at a perfume sample in the magazine. "I think I'll simply rely on my incredible memory."

"Rely on your memory for what?" Mr. Wakefield asked, coming into the den. He was carrying a stack of notepads and a fat law book bound in red leather.

"Oh, just a project for social studies," Jessica answered vaguely.

Mr. Wakefield settled into his favorite easy chair. "What kind of project?" he asked.

"We're keeping track of how we spend our time for an entire week, Dad," Elizabeth explained. "Things like eating, studying—"

"Magazine reading?" Mr. Wakefield broke in, giving Jessica a stern look.

Jessica closed her magazine guiltily. She could tell her father was still in a grumpy mood, and there was no point in aggravating him.

"You know, girls, keeping track of the hours he or she spends on a case is an important part of a lawyer's job. I have to keep very accurate records so I can bill my clients fairly," Mr. Wakefield said. "I can't just rely on my memory," he said, giving Jessica a meaningful look.

Jessica knew just where this conversation was going. Her father wanted her to get to work on the Hairnet's ridiculous project. She turned to Elizabeth. "Elizabeth, can I borrow a piece of notebook paper?" she asked.

"Sure." Elizabeth handed her several sheets and a pen.

Jessica looked up at her father to see if he was satisfied. To her surprise, he was already buried in his law book.

"Eight-thirty to eight thirty-five P.M.," she wrote at the top of her page. "Got yelled at by my father." *At the rate I'm going this week*, she thought miserably, *this probably won't be the last time I make an entry like this in my journal!*

Ten

◇

"Lizzie," Jessica said as she came into her sister's room later that night, "could you give me a hand with something?"

"These helping hands have helped all they're going to today," Elizabeth joked. She extended her palms for Jessica to examine. "I actually got blisters from mowing Mr. Caldwell's lawn! The next mowing job is all yours."

"That's why I need your help. If we can only win the radio contest, you'll never have to mow another lawn or wash another car," Jessica told her. "All we have to do is practice."

"Practice?" Elizabeth echoed. "How can you practice?"

"Come with me," Jessica said, grabbing her sister's arm. "I've got it all figured out."

Elizabeth let herself be pulled into Jessica's bedroom, where a stack of Johnny Buck albums was lying next to the stereo.

"You sit here," Jessica directed, holding out a chair for Elizabeth. "You're going to be the deejay."

"What?" Elizabeth asked in disbelief.

"You're going to be the deejay," Jessica repeated.

Elizabeth giggled. "If you say so."

Jessica ran over to her bed and sat on it cross-legged, with her back to Elizabeth. "Now, what I want you to do is put a record on the stereo. Any Johnny Buck album you like. You can play any song, and you can start anywhere in the song, but don't play more than a few seconds. I'll sit over here, looking the other way so I can't tell which album you picked."

"Do you really think this will help?"

"I'm sure of it." Jessica nodded enthusiastically. "Today I heard another contestant who only got *one* song right. I realized it would be a great idea to get used to listening to songs a little bit at a time. Now, go ahead and try me." She twisted around, adding as an afterthought, "But be careful with the needle. I don't want you to scratch my albums."

"OK. Here goes," Elizabeth said. She sorted through the stack until she found Johnny Buck's very first album, and gently set the record on the turntable.

". . . still missing you," Johnny Buck sang.

Elizabeth lifted the needle before he could sing the next line of the song. "Well, Jessica," she said, "can you name that song?"

" 'Long Time Gone'," Jessica answered, without a moment's hesitation.

Elizabeth consulted the album cover. "Wow!" she exclaimed. "How'd you do that?"

"I told you I could win the contest," Jessica said calmly. "Try another one."

This time Elizabeth picked a song she had never heard before. She set down the needle, and only four words played: "You're the one for . . ."

Jessica paused. This one was more difficult. She recognized the tune, but the words were unfamiliar.

"Can you name that song?" Elizabeth prompted.

Jessica frowned. Maybe this was going to be harder than she had thought it would be. "Wait a minute. . . . That's it!" she cried. " 'Hardhearted Love!' "

"Right again!"

Jessica turned around, beaming. "What did I tell you? All they have to do is call my name. I *know* I'll win!"

"Well, I hope they call your name soon," Elizabeth remarked. "Because Helping Hands has another job scheduled for tomorrow afternoon. Steven took the message while we were out working. Something about painting chairs."

"Painting?" Jessica fell back on the bed. "I *hate* to paint." She glanced over at the radio with a desperate expression. "That contest is our only hope!"

"How much did this lady say she'd pay us?" Jessica demanded as the twins trudged toward their latest job after school on Friday.

"She told Steven she'd give us fifteen dollars to paint four chairs," Elizabeth told her. "It sounds like a good deal."

"Nothing about Helping Hands is a good deal! I was supposed to go to Boosters practice this afternoon," Jessica pouted. "Instead, I'll be stuck at Mrs. Dithers'."

"Smithers," Elizabeth corrected her. "And you're not the only one who's making sacrifices. I've hardly had time to work on the newspaper at all this week. Poor Amy's been covering for me."

Jessica crossed her arms over her chest. "Well, all I can say is, I'm sick of being in business. I never realized work was . . . so much work!"

When the girls arrived at Mrs. Smithers', she led them to her backyard. There were four old wooden chairs placed on a large plastic drop cloth. She handed the girls a can of bright red paint and two paint brushes. "Try not to get this paint on you," she advised them. "It's awfully hard to get off."

While Jessica turned on her radio and adjusted her earphones, Elizabeth got to work. She had already painted the legs on the first chair when she noticed Jessica was nowhere in sight.

"Jessica!" Elizabeth called.

"Coming!" Jessica yelled back. She was at the far end of the yard, leaning over the white picket fence and staring very intently at something on the other side. Elizabeth stood up to get a better look, wondering what Jessica found so interesting.

"I should have known," Elizabeth muttered. It wasn't a *what*, it was a *who*. She watched as Jessica came dashing back across the yard.

"Did you see that guy weeding the lawn next door?" Jessica breathed.

"Not as well as *you* did," Elizabeth commented wryly as she handed her sister a paint brush.

Jessica unwillingly accepted the brush. She held the handle between her thumb and forefinger and wrinkled her nose. Then she dipped the brush into the can of paint, and made a few halfhearted swipes at one of the chairs.

"Ugh," she grumbled. "Why would anyone want to paint anything such a disgusting shade of red?"

Elizabeth began painting the seat of the chair she had been working on. "And to think Ellen Riteman wanted to change the Unicorns' official color to red!" Elizabeth said in mock horror.

Jessica didn't bother to respond. She was too busy spying on the boy next door. "How old do you think he is?" she asked in a low whisper.

Elizabeth shrugged. "Probably in high school."

"Well, I'm sure he was actually smiling at me a minute ago." Jessica set her brush down on the drop cloth and straightened her hair. "I'll be right back, Elizabeth."

"Jessica! You've only painted one leg!"

"I just want to get a little closer to see if I recognize him," she explained.

Elizabeth watched in amazement as Jessica walked back to the fence. When it came to squirming out of work, nobody was more inventive than her sister!

But the truth was, Elizabeth was just about as tired of Helping Hands as Jessica was. She knew there was no chance they would have five hundred dollars by the time Mr. Hopper came home. And Jessica's dream of winning the Name That Song Contest seemed highly unlikely. It was beginning to look like Jessica would have to confess.

Elizabeth was just closing up the paint can when Jessica returned, bubbling with excitement. "He's an eighth-grader, Lizzie. His name is Stu, and his family just moved here from Virginia!"

"That's nice," Elizabeth said flatly. The least Jessica could do was thank her for all her hard work!

But Jessica had apparently forgotten all about the chairs. "He's so cute I swear I'm going to faint," she declared dramatically.

Elizabeth watched silently as her sister sank onto the seat of the chair she had just finished painting.

"Boy, am I tired," Jessica continued. "Which is pretty silly, since all I've been doing is talking, while you've been painting."

Elizabeth bit her tongue to keep from laughing. "Don't worry," she managed. "I think there's one chair that needs a little touching up."

A look of horror slowly appeared on Jessica's face. "The chair!" she screeched, leaping up frantically. "I forgot it was wet!"

Jessica's back was covered with cherry-red paint from her shoulders to her knees. "Help me, Lizzie!" Jessica shrieked.

Elizabeth wanted to help, but she was laughing too hard. "Cheer up," she finally choked out. "Red really *is* your color."

"It'll never come off!" Jessica wailed pitifully.

"Maybe you can get the Unicorns to reconsider changing their official club color," Elizabeth suggested.

Jessica was not amused in the least.

"Hmm. What's that wonderful perfume you're wearing?" Elizabeth asked when Jessica joined her downstairs in the Wakefields' living room. "Turpentine cologne?"

Jessica had just emerged from the bathroom after what was probably the world's longest shower. She was more or less free of red paint.

"It's a good thing we had *something* that removed paint, or I'd still be as red as a lobster!"

Jessica laughed in spite of herself. "I looked like I had a sunburn on only one side!"

"Mrs. Smithers felt so bad about it, she actually gave us a five-dollar tip!"

"How much have we made altogether?" Jessica asked glumly as she sat next to Elizabeth on the couch. She knew it was a pretty safe bet that the grand total was not going to be earth-shaking.

Elizabeth counted off on her fingers. "Let's see," she said. "With ten dollars from Mrs. Leach yesterday, and twenty today, plus what we made before that . . . A grand total of forty-five dollars." She did her best to smile. "At this rate, we'll have the five hundred in about four months."

Jessica leaned back against the couch and closed her eyes.

"Jess?" Elizabeth ventured softly. "What are you thinking?"

"I'm thinking it's time to tell Dad the truth," Jessica said with a heavy sigh.

"There's always the radio contest," Elizabeth offered. She knew it was a long shot, but she wanted to say *something* hopeful. "They haven't called a contestant today."

Jessica shook her head. "It's no use, Elizabeth," she murmured. "I might as well get it over with. No matter how badly Dad punishes me, it can't be worse than working for Helping Hands!"

Outside, a car door slammed. Elizabeth peeked through the curtains to see who it was. "It can't be Dad," she pointed out. "He's in the kitchen." Her eyes lit up in sudden surprise. "Jessica!" she cried happily. "Mom's home!"

"But she wasn't supposed to get back until tomorrow!" Jessica said, jumping to her feet. She ran toward the front door, with Elizabeth close behind.

Mrs. Wakefield was just climbing out of the car when the twins rushed up to greet her, each taking one side to hug.

"What a wonderful welcoming committee!" she exclaimed, her blue eyes glowing.

"We've missed you!" Elizabeth cried.

"So, what did you bring us from San Francisco?" Jessica asked as she looped her arm around her mother's waist.

"What makes you think I brought you anything?" Mrs. Wakefield said with a smile.

"Because you're the greatest mom on earth, and I can't believe you wouldn't get me *something*!" Jessica responded.

"Besides," Elizabeth told her mother, "if you came home empty-handed, Jessica would pout for a week."

"Well, by amazing coincidence, it turns out I did get both of you something," Mrs. Wakefield said. "Some T-shirts that say San Francisco on them. Blue for you, Lizzie, and, of course, purple for Jessica."

"See, I told you you're the greatest mom on earth!" Jessica cried.

"Alice! You're home early!" Mr. Wakefield hurried out to the driveway, with Steven close on his heels.

"I finished up my meetings ahead of schedule and caught an early flight home," Mrs. Wakefield explained. She gave her husband a kiss and a long hug.

"Hey, Mom," Steven said, kissing his mother on the cheek. "Welcome home!"

"Does Steven get a T-shirt, too?" Jessica inquired.

"Just like yours, only an extra-large," Mrs. Wakefield answered, smiling. "How's everything been, Ned?" she asked her husband.

"Well, I've been working overtime on that brief I told you about. The house isn't too much of a disaster area, though," he added a little sheepishly.

Suddenly Jessica froze. She grabbed her sister's arm and held her back while the rest of the family went inside the house. "Oh, no!" she whispered frantically. "I completely forgot about the bathroom! It's a mess! You've got to help me, Lizzie! No matter what it takes, *stall Mom*. If she asks where I am, tell her I'm studying."

"She'll never believe that."

"OK, then, tell her I'm taking a shower. A very, very long shower." She gave Elizabeth a worried look. "I'm going to be up there a long time. There's red paint everywhere!"

"Use some of the cleanser under the sink," Elizabeth advised. "And hurry!"

Jessica rushed inside and sprinted toward the bathroom as if she were running the hundred-yard dash. As fast as she could, she piled all the dirty towels into one huge mound. The question was, what to do with them? Her bedroom seemed as good a hiding place as any. As Elizabeth had so kindly pointed out, you could safely hide an elephant in there.

Jessica was stuffing the last towel under her bed when she heard Steven's voice.

"You've got your work cut out for you," he said sarcastically, leaning in her doorway.

"Beat it, Steven," Jessica snapped. "I'm kind of busy, if you don't mind."

"*I'll* say," he said with obvious amusement.

"What happened to your bathroom, anyway? It looks like a scene from a horror movie."

"That's red paint, if you must know." Jessica rushed back to the bathroom and began searching for a sponge. "Not that it's any of your business."

Steven continued to watch Jessica while she began frantically scrubbing the bathtub. "You've got to be setting some kind of record," he marveled. "I wonder if the Olympics has a speed-cleaning event?"

"Would you please get lost?" Jessica seethed. "Permanently?"

"You missed a spot," Steven remarked over his shoulder before heading downstairs.

For the next five minutes Jessica continued her scrubbing, silently wondering why she always waited until the last minute to do everything. She just ended up working twice as hard trying to get things done in half the time.

She paused for a moment, surveying the bathroom critically. Well, at least she had made a little progress. As long as Elizabeth continued to stall their mother, she might actually get this done.

"How's it going?"

Jessica glanced up from her work on the tub to see Elizabeth smiling sympathetically. "Lizzie!" she cried. "What about Mom?"

"She's having coffee with Dad in his study. I figured it was safe to come up and give you a pep talk."

Just then Steven reappeared. "Jessica," he called over Elizabeth's shoulder, "I hate to interrupt when you're having so much fun—"

"Steven, would you stop bugging me?" Jessica demanded in frustration.

"I just wanted to let you know that you're supposed to call some guy named Hal."

"Hal?" Jessica echoed. "I don't know anybody named Hal." She peered at Steven more closely. He had a very strange grin plastered on his face.

"He said you had five minutes to call back."

Five minutes? Jessica wondered. *What kind of a person would only give you five minutes to call back?*

Then it dawned on her. "The contest!" she screamed, throwing her sponge in the air and rushing over to give Elizabeth a hug. "When did you hear?"

"After I said hi to Mom, I stopped by the kitchen to get something to eat. I turned on the radio, and this announcer was saying, 'Jessica Wakefield, you have five minutes to call your pal Hal at KSVR and play Name That Song!' I figured I should go ahead and tell you, since, if you win, you'll undoubtedly want to share the prize with your favorite brother."

Jessica charged into the hallway. "The phone!" she cried. "I've got to call them right away!"

"Now, calm down," Elizabeth shouted. "You're going to have to concentrate, Jess."

"I know, I know," Jessica said impatiently. "But don't worry. You saw how good I am at this." With a confident smile, she picked up the telephone. But before she could dial, her grin evaporated. Her father was talking on the other extension, and it sounded like a long-distance call.

"Elizabeth!" she hissed. "Dad's using the phone! And this is our one big chance!"

Eleven

◇

"Do something, Lizzie!" she pleaded.

"What?" Elizabeth asked helplessly.

"Something! Anything!" Jessica wailed. "Just get him off the phone!"

Without another word, Elizabeth dashed down the stairs. Steven looked at Jessica and shrugged. "Sorry, kid," he said. "I'd stay to give you moral support, but I wouldn't miss this for the world." He galloped down the stairs.

Elizabeth approached her father's study cautiously, wracking her brain for a way to get him off the phone. When Steven appeared behind her, she whispered, "As soon as he hangs up, run up and tell Jessica."

"Gotcha." Steven nodded. "But what are you going to tell him?"

"I don't know yet," Elizabeth answered anxiously as she knocked gently on the half-open study door.

"What is it, honey?" Mrs. Wakefield asked in a low whisper. "Dad's on the phone."

"I . . . I need to talk to him right away," Elizabeth stammered.

"Maybe I can help you," her mother offered.

"No, Mom. I need to know if I can use the phone."

"Can't it wait?"

"It's really, really important," Elizabeth insisted. "Please?"

Mrs. Wakefield signaled to her husband. "Ned?" she said softly. "Elizabeth says she needs to use the phone."

Mr. Wakefield grimaced. "Jack, can I call you right back?" he said into the receiver. "Looks like we've got ourselves a little phone emergency."

As soon as he hung up the phone, Elizabeth nodded to Steven, who went dashing back up the stairs to tell Jessica the coast was clear.

"Do you mind telling me what's so important that it had to interrupt my business call?" Mr. Wakefield demanded.

"Well . . ." Elizabeth chewed on her lower lip. *Think of something!* she told herself. "The person I have to call is only going to be there for a few more minutes."

"And it's really that important?" Mr. Wakefield asked.

Elizabeth nodded.

"You've got five minutes, Elizabeth," her father said, sighing. "But don't let this happen again. Understand?"

"I promise," Elizabeth said sincerely. She rushed upstairs to the hallway. "All clear!" she told Jessica.

"I know," Jessica answered as she continued dialing. "Steven told me."

While Elizabeth and Steven watched nervously, Jessica listened to the phone ring. "They're not answering!" she moaned. "I hope it's not too late."

Suddenly her eyes opened wide as she heard the deejay's voice on the other end. "Is this lucky Jessica Wakefield?" he asked.

"Um, yes," Jessica answered shakily.

"How old are you, Jessica?"

"I'm twelve," she said.

"And where do you go to school?"

"I go to Sweet Valley Middle School."

"OK, Jessica Wakefield of Sweet Valley Middle School, are you ready to play Name That Song?" The deejay's voice was very loud. He was making Jessica a little nervous.

"Yes. I guess so."

"Then here's your first song!"

Jessica heard a few seconds of music in the telephone receiver. It was an easy one.

"That's 'Saturday Blues,' " Jessica said confidently.

"Yes!" the deejay shouted. "One down, and four more to go!"

The next two were harder, but Jessica got them after a few moments of hesitation. The one after that was easy, and she guessed it instantly.

At last they were down to the final song. One more and she would have the thousand dollars!

"Are you ready for the fifth and final song, Jessica?" the deejay asked.

"Yes," she replied nervously.

As soon as she heard the music, Jessica smiled. *This* one was easier than any of the others. It was "A Dozen Bucks," definitely one of Johnny Buck's best songs.

In a few more seconds, she'd have a thousand bucks and all of her worries would be over!

"Can you name that song?" the deejay demanded.

"Yes," Jessica answered excitedly. "It's 'A Thousand Bucks'!"

"No!" the deejay shouted. "Oh, and you were

so close, Jessica! The song was 'A *Dozen* Bucks,' the title cut off one of Johnny's best-selling albums! Not a thousand, just a dozen! Sorry, my friend."

Jessica dropped the receiver down, a stunned expression on her face.

"Well?" Elizabeth demanded, afraid to hear the answer.

"I blew it!" Jessica wailed. "My big chance, and I blew it!" She looked at Elizabeth with disbelief in her eyes. "I was doing so well, Lizzie. Just like when we practiced. But then I got to the last song—"

"And what?" Elizabeth asked impatiently.

"And I knew it. It was 'A Dozen Bucks'—"

"But you *said* a thousand . . ." Elizabeth trailed off.

"It just sort of came out." Jessica plopped down wearily on the floor.

"Tough luck, shrimp," Steven said sympathetically. "There'll be other contests."

"Not in time to do *me* any good," Jessica said glumly.

"Are you off the phone yet, Elizabeth?" It was Mrs. Wakefield, coming up the stairway.

"Yes, Mom," Elizabeth answered. "Thank you. I was just coming down to tell you we—I—was done."

"Boy, are we *ever* done," Jessica whispered.

Mrs. Wakefield reached the top of the stairs and peered into the twins' bathroom. "Well, well," she said. "I guess I should go away more often. I don't think I've ever seen your bathroom look cleaner. Good work, girls. I'm proud of you."

Not for long, Jessica thought sullenly.

The next morning when Jessica woke up, she knew the time she had been dreading for so long had finally arrived. It was a Saturday, but she had heard her dad say he was going to have to go in to work for at least part of the day. Outside, the weather was gloomy, just like Jessica's mood.

She dressed slowly and tried to plan what she was going to say to her father. But no matter how long she practiced, she would never find an easy way to say "I've lost the five hundred dollars."

Jessica headed down the stairs. She went to her father's study, but he wasn't there and his briefcase was gone. Maybe she was off the hook, for the morning, at least.

But she hadn't heard her father's car start up yet. She headed down the hall and into the living room just in time to catch sight of her father.

He snatched his jacket off the couch and dashed toward the front door. He was obviously in a hurry.

Jessica thought she saw something fall out of his jacket pocket and onto the floor. "Dad?" she said, just softly enough so she could be certain he couldn't hear her.

The front door closed behind him, and a moment later Jessica heard his car engine rumbling.

"Oh, well," she murmured. "At least I tried." She wandered into the living room, where her eyes landed on a folded brown envelope on the floor. It was probably the thing she had seen fall out of her father's jacket when he grabbed it off the couch.

She stooped down to pick it up, and suddenly her heart did a flip-flop. The writing in the corner of the envelope read, "J. Hopper, Thirty-seven Walnut Street"!

Holding her breath, Jessica reached inside the envelope. There in the bottom was a thick wad of money. Five hundred dollars, to be exact. Her father had the money all along!

Jessica didn't know whether to laugh or cry. She danced up the stairway to Elizabeth's room, bursting in without even knocking.

"Jessica!" Elizabeth said in surprise as she combed her hair back into a neat ponytail. "I was just going to come looking for you. I have wonderful news!" She could barely control her excitement.

"So have I!" Jessica cried.

"I've solved the mystery of the missing money!" Elizabeth announced proudly.

"So have I!" Jessica replied. She paused suddenly, giving Elizabeth a quizzical look as she hid the envelope behind her back. "Wait a minute. How could *you* have solved the mystery?"

Elizabeth tapped her index finger on her head. "By using my brain, naturally," she said with a cocky smile. "How did *you* figure out who had the money?"

"You tell me first," Jessica responded craftily.

"Well, I finished my mystery novel last night," Elizabeth explained, tying a blue ribbon around her ponytail. "And I finally figured out who the villain was. It was the butler."

Jessica sat down on Elizabeth's bed, smiling politely. The envelope was still behind her back. "I thought the butler *always* did it."

"But he was so obviously the bad guy, I just assumed it had to be someone else," Elizabeth continued.

"Go on," Jessica said.

"So, I started thinking about the missing money, and how we were trying so hard to come up with an explanation. The answer is so obvious, we forgot to consider it. Fortunately," Elizabeth smiled, "with my amazing skill at solving mysteries, I've finally solved the case!"

"OK, Amanda," Jessica teased. "Who has the money?"

"Steven!" Elizabeth announced confidently.

"*Steven?*" Jessica howled. "Are you nuts?" She dissolved into giggles.

"Jessica, it *has* to be him," Elizabeth argued. "My guess is that the money somehow fell out of the racket cover when Steven was cleaning out the utility closet. He must have accidentally picked up the envelope and moved it to his bedroom, with all his other junk. I'm sure the money's in there right now."

"No, it's not," Jessica said with a secret smile.

"How do you know?" Elizabeth asked.

"Because I have it right here!" Jessica cried. She handed the envelope to her sister.

"Jess!" Elizabeth said in amazement. "The money!" She gave Jessica a hug. "But where did you ever find it?"

"You'll never believe it. Dad had it. The envelope fell out of his jacket this morning, and I found it on the living room floor."

"I guess I'm not such a hot detective, after all," Elizabeth said quietly.

"I think you were on the right track, Lizzie.

Dad probably found the money when he opened the closet and the racket fell on his head."

"But why didn't he tell you?" Elizabeth demanded.

Jessica shrugged. "Maybe he forgot about it. He's been so busy this week. Or maybe he figured out that I didn't deliver the money like I promised, and he decided to teach me a lesson."

"Well, the important thing is, your problems are over," Elizabeth said with a relieved sigh. "Now you can straighten things out with Dad."

Jessica smiled. There was a mischievous gleam in her blue-green eyes. "And just maybe teach *him* a little lesson, too!"

Twelve

◇

That evening Mr. Wakefield arrived home looking and sounding like a new man.

"I want to apologize to you kids," he told them. "I realize I've been kind of an ogre all week. I guess I've had a lot on my mind. I'm sure you'll all be relieved to hear that my project is finally finished."

Jessica sneaked out of the room and returned a moment later with the money behind her back. "Speaking of apologies," she said, trying to sound tearful, "I'm afraid I have an *awful* confession to make." She caught Elizabeth's eye and swallowed a giggle. "I lost Mr. Hopper's five hundred dollars, Dad."

Her father smiled smugly. "You did, did you?"

He stood, and suddenly his expression clouded. "Now what did I do with that?" he muttered under his breath. "Was it in my office?" He headed toward the hallway. "Just a second, Jess," he called over his shoulder. "I'm just trying to remember where I—"

"Try your jacket, Dad," Jessica offered.

"Oh, that's right." He smiled again, reaching into his jacket pocket. When he realized the money was no longer there, his voice grew anxious. "I could have sworn . . ." he grumbled. He looked closely at Jessica. "Wait a minute. Jessica—"

Before he could say anything more, she handed her father the envelope. "It fell out of your jacket this morning," she explained.

Mr. Wakefield's eyes darkened, and for a second Jessica was afraid he was mad at her. But then he broke into a grin.

"Jessica," he said in an apologetic tone, "I'm very sorry. When I found that money in the racket cover I stuck it in my jacket pocket. I meant to discuss it with you that night, but I've been so busy, I completely forgot about it. And I haven't worn this jacket all week."

Jessica shared a smile with Elizabeth.

"Of course, you should have delivered that money promptly," he continued in a sterner tone. "But I don't want you to *ever* feel you have to hide your mistakes from your mom and me. No matter what, it's always best to come to us, and we'll work it out together. That's what we're here for."

"I know, Dad," Jessica said, giving him a hug. "I guess I just wasn't thinking."

"So what else is new?" Steven piped up.

Jessica ignored her brother. "If you like," she told her father, "I'll take the money over as soon as Mr. Hopper gets back. It's the least I can do."

Elizabeth and Mrs. Wakefield exchanged meaningful looks. "All things considered," Mrs. Wakefield said, "maybe Elizabeth and I should deliver the money."

"I suppose you have a point," Jessica said, laughing good-naturedly. "Although Lizzie's already done enough for one week!"

"Funny you should mention that, Jess," Elizabeth said with a sly grin. She retrieved her backpack and pulled out a blue notebook. "I've been doing a little figuring in my time-use journal, and I've come to some pretty interesting conclusions. You'll never guess how I spent the largest percentage of my time this week. Besides sleeping and going to school, that is."

"Let's see," Jessica mused. "Studying?"

Elizabeth shook her head.

"Showering?" Steven volunteered.

"Nope," Elizabeth said.

"Reading would be my guess," said Mr. Wakefield.

"Wrong again," Elizabeth said. "So far this week I've spent twenty-one percent of my time helping you out, Jessica!" she announced with a laugh.

"You're kidding!" Jessica exclaimed. "Of course, what are sisters for?" she asked quickly. "You got the pleasure of my company, after all. And don't forget the forty-five dollars we have to show for all our hard work!" She paused for a moment. "You know what, Lizzie?" she said thoughtfully. "I've got a great idea for a way to spend that money."

"I'll bet it involves purple clothes," Steven teased.

"As a matter of fact," Jessica retorted, "it involves something pink." She smiled at Elizabeth. "A new pink blouse, to be exact. Seems to me it's the least I can do to pay you back for taking up twenty-one percent of your time. Plus"—she paused to do some quick calculating—"I should have enough left over for those silver earrings I've been wanting to buy."

"Maybe we can go to the mall later," Elizabeth said with a grin.

By Monday, Jessica had practically forgotten all about her problems with the missing money. Unfortunately, it seemed like everyone at school had heard about her near miss with the Name That Song Contest, and nobody was about to let her forget it!

"Hey, Jessica, I heard this great new Johnny Buck song on the radio this weekend," Ellen Riteman said as they headed down the hall between classes.

Jessica rolled her eyes toward the ceiling. She had heard this joke a million times today.

"And guess what it was called?" Ellen continued. " 'A Thousand Bucks'!"

"She got four out of five songs right, Ellen," Elizabeth said, rushing to her sister's defense. "That's better than most people do."

"Well, at least she won't go around with her radio on all the time anymore," Lila commented. She still hadn't forgiven Jessica for saying she weighed a ton in front of a crowd of people.

Before Jessica could answer, a boy came tearing down the hallway, nearly knocking her over.

"Who on earth was that?" Jessica demanded.

"Danny Jackson," Lila said. "Are you OK?"

"Yeah, but he nearly ran me over."

"Did you hear what he did today during English class?" Lila asked.

"No, what?" Jessica asked. At least they had dropped the subject of the radio contest.

"They got a pop quiz, and instead of taking it, Danny made his test paper into an airplane and tossed it out the window! Can you believe it?"

"He's always getting into trouble," Ellen agreed.

"I wonder what would make him act that way?" Elizabeth wondered aloud.

"It's really too bad," Ellen said. "He's one of the best runners Sweet Valley Middle School's ever had."

"Well, I'll tell you one thing. If Danny Jackson keeps getting into trouble, he won't be on the track team much longer!" Jessica predicted.

Will Danny get thrown off the track team? Find out in Sweet Valley Twins #40, **Danny Means Trouble**.

☐	15681-0	**TEAMWORK #27**	$2.75
☐	15688-8	**APRIL FOOL! #28**	$2.75
☐	15695-0	**JESSICA AND THE BRAT ATTACK #29**	$2.75
☐	15715-9	**PRINCESS ELIZABETH #30**	$2.75
☐	15727-2	**JESSICA'S BAD IDEA #31**	$2.75
☐	15747-7	**JESSICA ON STAGE #32**	$2.75
☐	15753-1	**ELIZABETH'S NEW HERO #33**	$2.75
☐	15766-3	**JESSICA, THE ROCK STAR #34**	$2.75
☐	15772-8	**AMY'S PEN PAL #35**	$2.75
☐	15778-7	**MARY IS MISSING #36**	$2.75
☐	15779-5	**THE WAR BETWEEN THE TWINS #37**	$2.75
☐	15789-2	**LOIS STRIKES BACK #38**	$2.75
☐	15798-1	**JESSICA AND THE MONEY MIX-UP #39**	$2.75
☐	15806-6	**DANNY MEANS TROUBLE #40**	$2.75
☐	15810-4	**THE TWINS GET CAUGHT #41**	$2.75
☐	15824-4	**JESSICA'S SECRET #42**	$2.95
☐	15835-X	**ELIZABETH'S FIRST KISS #43**	$2.95

Bantam Books, Dept. SVT5, 414 East Golf Road, Des Plaines, IL 60016

Please send me the items I have checked above. I am enclosing $_____
(please add $2.00 to cover postage and handling). Send check or money
order, no cash or C.O.D.s please.

Mr/Ms ――――――――――――――――――――――――

Address ――――――――――――――――――――――――

City/State ―――――――――――――― Zip ――――――――

SVT5-11/90

Please allow four to six weeks for delivery.
Prices and availability subject to change without notice.